OUTBREAK

By

E.T. Jahn

Published by **Mandrill**
A division of Trident Media Company
801 N Pitt Street, Suite 123
Alexandria, VA 22314 USA

Dedication

This book is dedicated to my wife and family in gratitude for their unwavering support and encouragement.

I also wish to extend a special thanks to all of the devoted doctors, nurses, and health professionals that helped me in the development of this novel.

Prologue

Driven by the demands of an exploding population, scientists have embarked on many new and sometimes far reaching projects. In an effort to expand the world's food supply, researchers have begun to alter the formulas at the foundation of life itself, resulting in marked controversy. Of all the challenges faced by the worldwide medical community, genetic engineering is one of the most controversial.

Over the years the possibility it presents has captured man's imagination. For each new accomplishment there is the prospect of a new and often unexpected situation.

Although this story and its characters are fictional, it illustrates the need to recognize that even the most well- meaning efforts could create an violent and uncontrolled. . . Overload.

Even though the federal government continually upgrades testing standards for meat and poultry products, recent statistics indicate that several million people are made ill each year from food-related illnesses directly linked to food contaminants produced by bacteria or other micro-organisms.Another nine thousand people die.

Chapter 1

Day 1

Piedmont Medical Center

Emergency Room

Doctor Wayne Collins the chief of emergency medicine for the past five years, looked around at the empty beds and hoped that they would stay that way. A soft-spoken man with a square jaw and cool gray eyes, he had served in the Mideast with an army medical unit during Desert Storm. He felt that the experience had taught him more about treating and understanding human trauma than all of his medical school training. This knowledge continued to be invaluable to him upon his return to Virginia to work in Emergency Medicine at the Medical Center.

He continually sought to bring out the best in his people. Most of the staff knew he was more astute than his quiet mannerisms suggested. As he walked toward the nurses' station he was paged to report to the Medical Command Center.

He passed the examining areas that lined the Emergency Room. Each cubicle contained an EKG monitor, a blood pressure stand, and an oxygen hookup, plus other equipment used during emergencies. He continued on to the far end of the room, where the Medical Command Center was located. Here all emergency calls coming in from medical units were handled. He paused beside Meg Walden, the charge nurse.

"Med-Flight One is approaching the pad with a working code," she said, turning from the dispatcher. Collins moved closer to the radio console and listened to the incoming message.

"Medical Command, Med-Flight One with an update."

Picking up the microphone, Collins depressed the button.

"Med-Flight One, this is Doctor Collins, go ahead, please."

"Yes, sir, we are two minutes out. We have a working code in progress for three minutes. We have the patient intubated and we're bagging him. CPR is in progress, copy?"

"That's affirmative, Med-flight One. We'll be waiting for you." Turning to Walden he said, "Have room one set up for a CODE BLUE and get everyone in place. I'm going out to meet the chopper," and he left the Medical Command Center.

In the hallway he saw two orderlies talking. "Bring that Gurney and come with me," he ordered.

They went out to the black top landing pad located across from the small parking area directly opposite the ER entrances. The helicopter touched down, and Collins and the orderlies moved forward. With the rotor blades still turning, the crew carefully removed the patient and transferred him to the waiting Gurney. "Okay, whom do we have?" he asked.

The flight nurse replied, "We have Bob Warren. He is a white male, thirty-eight years old, approximately one hundred eighty-five pounds. He initially presented with a severe headache, fever, and intense abdominal pain and nausea. No known previous medical history. He arrested approximately seven minutes ago."

They arrived at the emergency room that only a short time ago had been quiet and was now brightly lit and filled with a full working team of nurses and respiratory therapists.

Collins took the call sheet as the team continued to administer CPR.

The flight nurse continued, "He went into in Vfib, with no pressure. We administered fifty mg of Lidocaine IV bolus and have an IV of normal saline running wide open. We also have two ambulances en route with three members of this man's family."

"Great!" Collins said and turned to Meg Walden. "Give an amp of epinephrine and stand clear to shock." Walden administered the epinephrine and stood back.

"Clear!" he shouted as he looked down the table, and then hit the paddles. They watched as the electrical charge caused the body to jump. Looking up at the EKG monitor, Doctor Collins again saw no response. Increasing the electrical charge, he again called, "Clear!" and placed the paddles on the patient's chest. He saw no response and ordered, "Another ampule of epinephrine and resume compressions." The therapist continued to ventilate every five seconds.

"He's not responding; doctor, he's still flat line," called the therapist. Additional doses of medication were administered but with no response. "What's the down time?" Collins asked, looking up at the respiratory therapist.

"Forty-five minutes," she replied.

Collins turned from the table and wiped his face on his sleeve. "Call it at twenty hundred hours." Gazing around the room he saw the look of frustration on the faces of the code team, one he'd seen many times before. He too felt a sense of loss.

"Notify the morgue, tell them I'd like to get an autopsy started as soon we get authorization from the family. And let them know we have three more patients on the way in, apparently with the same symptoms." He had been warned of this while striving to save Warren's life. He walked to the sink, removed his gloves, and washed his hands methodically. The deceased patient was covered and tagged, in preparation for removal to the morgue.

The phone rang; Meg Walden picked up the receiver and listened. She turned to Collins and said, "Doctor the squad just called in. They have an ETA of five minutes and they say Mr. Warren's wife is the worst, she's convulsing as he did before he arrested."

"Set up rooms two, three, and four," he ordered. "We may have three more codes in here in the next few minutes." He finished drying his hands, tossed the towel into the linen waste container, and walked back to the desk.

"Right away, doctor," she replied and hurriedly left to make the preparations.

"Oh, boy," Collins said, looking at the death certificate for

Bob Warren. He checked the time on the wall clock and wondered what to put down as the cause of death.

By the time Meg Walden returned, the two rescue units had arrived. "Doctor, the rest of the Warren family are here. The wife is critical. They're putting her in room two. The others, I believe, a sister and her husband, are also running high fevers."

"I'm on my way," he said as he placed the uncompleted death certificate on the desk. "I'll examine the wife first, and I want a full set of vitals on the other two. After examining them, maybe we'll have a clue of what caused Warren's death. I'll also need blood cultures, CRC, 02 SATs, and a tox screen. Get the samples to the lab as soon as they draw the blood. Oh, and have them take chest x-rays, just in case they've ingested anything."

"Yes, doctor," she said.

Collins entered the examining room and looked down at Sue Warren. She was only thirty-five years old, but long hours helping her husband maintain their small chicken farm made her look ten years older. Her long mousy brown hair was tied back with a rubber band and her bangs were plastered to her forehead as perspiration ran down the sides of her face that was etched in pain. Her clothes had been removed and replaced with a white hospital gown. As he began his examination she held her stomach and pulled her legs into the fetal position. The deep chills brought on by the high fever caused her body to shake uncontrollably.

"They're on the way from the lab," Meg said approaching Collins.

He leaned over and placed a stethoscope on Sue Warren's chest. Looking up he said, "Her heart rate is 150 and irregular, and she just had a short seizure. Set up an EKG and chest X-ray stat. I want her vitals checked every five minutes. I also want you to give her a gram of Dilantin IV drip in 250 cc normal saline over thirty minutes." He moved a small pen light from left to right across the patient's eyes. "Until we know what we're dealing with, I want everyone involved with these patients to exercise full precautions--gowns, masks, gloves, the works. Let me know if she's able give you any information about what brought on this illness," he said, and left the examining room. He walked back to the center of the thirty-bed emergency facility that was divided into specialized treatment areas. The first five rooms were set up to treat high priority patients such as cardiac or related conditions. In addition there were trauma rooms, pediatric, and general illness rooms.

He glanced up at the grease board located behind the nurses' station and checked for the on-call attending neurologist. Picking up the telephone he dialed the operator. "This is Doctor Collins. Please page Doctor Bennett and have him call me in the ER, stat."

He replaced the receiver and looked up to see Andy Frame. A second-year resident, Frame was completing his three-month rotation in the emergency room. Like most residents he essentially lived at the hospital and spent most of his waking hours on duty. At twenty-seven, he was three years from completing his training.

"I hope you got some rest," Collins said, watching as the younger man buttoned his lab coat, pushed back his light brown hair, and adjusted his glasses.

"I got an hour more than usual. Will that help?" Frame asked, hanging a stethoscope around his neck. "Looks like it might be an interesting night."

"Looks that way. So far I have one thirty-eight-year-old white male in the morgue, his wife in room two in critical condition, and two more members of the family in rooms three and four, presenting with similar symptoms. I was just on my way in to examine them."

"Do you have any idea what's wrong with them?" Frame asked as they walked toward the examining rooms.

"Not yet. It could be any number of things, botulism, maybe meningitis, possibly some kind of fumes. I'm having the lab run the blood work and tox screen, and I have a call in for Doctor Bennett in neurology.

"I want to get spinal taps done and we'll see if that gives us anything. Whatever it is seems to be affecting the sympathetic system. We might even be looking at some type of central nervous system (CNS) infection. They all have high fevers, severe abdominal pain, diarrhea, nausea, and rapid heart rates. They're all likely to code if we don't slow down whatever this is."

They walked to the examining area where a staff nurse called, "Doctor Collins, Doctor Bennett is on line two for you."

"Andy, while I talk to Charlie Bennett, I'd like you to examine the patient in room four. When I'm through with this call I'll check the patient in room three. Then we can compare notes and see what we come up with. And, Andy, pay particular attention to any distinct odors or stains that might be on the clothing, or any unusual marks such as snake or insect bites. If we're dealing with some kind of contaminant, it may give us a clue as to what it is."

"Okay, on my way," Frame said as he headed for room four.

"Thanks," Collins said as he picked up the phone next to him. "Charlie, I'm glad you're still here. Listen, we have something going on down here that could get messy. I need your neurological expertise, spinal taps, and a CT scan on three patients."

"I'll arrange for it, Wayne," replied Bennett. "What do you have?"

"All I can tell you is they're all from the same family, were taken from the same house, and for the most part are presenting in the same manner. I'll fill you in when you get here."

"I'll be right down, Wayne."

Collins had met Charlie Bennett eight months ago when he joined the hospital staff as chief resident of neurology. Bennett left a promising career in New York and accepted the offer from the center in hopes that the stress of his wife's late-term pregnancy would be easier to deal with in a less populated area. Concern for her health was keeping Bennett preoccupied and Collins hoped that this added workload would not affect his performance.

Entering room four Andy removed the chart from the foot of the bed and read it. Ellen Evans, age thirty, married, no known

PMH available. Chief complaint, severe abdominal pain, chills, and nausea. He replaced the chart and looked at the nurse who was monitoring the patient and asked, "Has she been able to tell you anything?"

"No, doctor. She's been pretty incoherent since she arrived. I don't believe we have gotten any information from any of them."

"Too bad," he said continuing the examination. A few minutes later Collins entered the room. "This young lady is in a bad way," Frame said. "Her fever is 105, her heart rate is 140, and she convulsed heavily. We have her in the cold blanket, and I have a normal saline IV running. I also gave her a gram of Dilantin IV. The acetaminophen suppositories should have brought down the fever, but so far nothing seems to be helping."

"We have the same thing in the other room, Andy. I just gave her husband a Digitalis IV slow push and set up a drip. I want to stop those convulsions and try to stabilize their heart rate. If we can stabilize one of them long enough to talk to us, we might have some idea of what caused this." Just then the distinctive sound of ambulance sirens pierced the night air. "Boy, I hope that's not more of the same," Collins said. Before he could comment further, he was called to the Medical Command Center.

"It's getting worse," said Walden as Collins and Frame approached. "We have two more patients on the way in, with the same symptoms as the first four."

"Are they related to the first group?" Collins asked.

"No," Walden replied. "The ambulance crew asked the same question, and they say there appears to be no obvious connection except that they live about a mile apart."

"I don't know what we've got going here, but let's not take any chances," Collins said. "Meg, call the ICU units, find out how many beds we have available, and ask them to hold everything they can. I also want a count on respirators. Then get a hold of Doctor Lane; she's the anesthesia attending. Oh, and call the nursing supervisor; tell her what we have. If this keeps up I'll need her to activate the emergency response plan. I want to be sure she has all the information she'll need."

"I'll check and get back to you as soon as I hear," she said.

Collins turned to a staff nurse and said, "Call security; tell them I want this section of the ER quarantined. Have them direct any other unit arriving with patients presenting with similar symptoms through the back entrance, so we can establish a clean zone."

"I'll get right on it, doctor." Looking up at him she asked, "Do you really think it might be that bad?"

He knew what she was thinking. "I honestly don't know, but I have a hunch this is going to be one very long shift," he said, and headed for the receiving area as the ER doors burst open and two stretchers were rolled in.

Chapter 2

Day I

Piedmont Medical Center

Doctor Charlie Bennett and his team were preparing the last of the three patients for a spinal tap. The nurse positioned Ellen Evans on her side in readiness for the tap. Bennett observed that this patient, like the first two, had poor color and had been perspiring profusely. Noting these conditions, he had first thought that they might have been caused by an insect or snake bite, but neither the medical nor neurological examinations had shown any physical signs of these.

The spinal tap was ordered to obtain a sample of cerebrospinal fluid, often vital in confirming a diagnosis. The fluid shows certain characteristics when specific diseases affecting the brain or spinal cord are present. A rise in pressure can indicate the presence of any number of life-threatening conditions such as brain tumors, cerebral hemorrhage, acute meningitis, and other infections.

The patient was placed on her left side with her legs drawn up to her chest. Her back was exposed, and Bennett administered a local anesthetic. He then carefully inserted a long thin needle through the draped window, penetrating through the vertebra interspace and into the subarachnoid space of her lumbar spine. He withdrew the metal stylet, and clear liquid started to flow.

Continuing, he inserted the catheter (a tube that was connected to a manometer) to take a pressure reading on the spinal fluid. This completed, he partially filled four small vials with fluid for microscopic, chemical, and bacterial analysis. He then carefully compared the color of all four samples. When he had finished, the nurse who had been holding Ellen during the procedure, placed her in a prone position on the bed. Bennett stepped away from the table. Pushing his rimless glasses up on his forehead, he rubbed the bridge of his nose. "Get these to the lab right away. Take her upstairs," he said to the nurse, "and stay with her."

"Yes, doctor," she said and wheeled Ellen from the room.

Removing his glasses he stepped to the sink, washed his hands, and splashed water on his face. Glancing into the small mirror over the sink he sighed. Where did all this gray come from? Seemed the last time he looked he had a full head of blonde hair. He was about to leave the room when Wayne Collins walked in.

"How is it going, Charlie?" Collins asked.

"We just finished the last tap. The fluid was clear, and the pressure was just slightly above normal. I'll know more when I get the lab report. What's the situation out front?"

"Not good. We have had two more brought in exhibiting the same symptoms. We have IVs running on all of them, and we're giving them an anticonvulsant and acetaminophen to try and reduce the fever."

"Has there been any change?"

"No, Charlie, nothing seems to be working. The worst part of it is we don't even know what brought this on. For now, I'm just trying to cover all the bases. I've asked them to call the night shift and have them come in early. At the rate patients are arriving, we're going to need more hands than we have now. By the way, I have a call in for Laura Stewart from the Infectious Disease Unit. I want to get her in here and see if she can make some sense of this."

"Good," Bennett replied. "The CT scans they ran showed normal intra cranial pressure which were backed up by taps. We can review the results with her when she arrives. I'll be in the clinical bacteriological lab. I want to call Amanda and see how she's doing. You know she's due any time now."

"Look, Charlie, I know this pregnancy has you and Amanda

upset. If you want I can ask Doctor Fry to cover this for you."

"No! Wayne. I'll be okay. It'll give me something else to focus on. But thanks anyway, I appreciate it. I'll let you know what the lab comes up with."

"Thanks, Charlie. Give Amanda my regards. As soon as Laura gets here, I'll get everyone together and go over what we have and where we go next." Collins started to leave the room, but stopped abruptly, and listened to the voice on the paging system. "CODE BLUE, room two, CODE BLUE TEAM, room two. Doctor Collins to room two stat."

"Damn!" he said and raced out the door.

When he entered the room Meg Walden looked up as she moved the crash cart into position. "It's Mrs. Warren, doctor. She was in V-fib. We administered Lidocaine, but now she's asystole."

Sue Warren lay unmoving on the bed. Collins grabbed a pair of sterile gloves from the cabinet and placed the chest and back pads of an external transthoracic pacemaker on the patient in an attempt to reinitiate cardiac rhythm. The medical team stood by to assist.

"Epi, doctor?" Walden asked.

"Give it."

Walden injected a syringe of epinephrine, a cardiac stimulant into the IV.

"Atropine?"

"Give it." The same procedure was followed.

"Atropine and epi given, doctor."

"Continue CPR," called Collins. Watching the monitor, he said, "Give me the time."

"Ten minutes, sir."

"Stop compressions," Collins instructed, watching the monitor for any change. He looked toward Walden, who was holding new syringes of epi and atropine.

"Give it," he said.

"Epi and atropine given, doctor."

"She's still flat line," called the therapist who had been ventilating her.

"Continue compressions," Collins ordered. "Meg, give me another amp of epi for an intra cardiac injection, stat."

Walden prepared the cardiac needle and passed it to him. She stepped aside and watched as he injected the syringe into the patient's chest between the ribs, just left of the sternum, drew back slightly to test his positioning, then injected the epi directly into the heart.

His attention focused on the cardiac monitor, he watched with the team for any sign of change. He checked for a pulse at the carotid artery, located on either side of the neck. Feeling no pulse, he gently lifted the woman's eyelids. Her pupils were fully dilated, indicating that all life functions had ceased and the eye's ciliary muscle had fully relaxed. Closing the eyelids, he said without looking up. "Time."

"Thirty minutes, doctor," was the response. "Are you calling the code, sir?"

"Yes, call it 22:30 hours."

"I'll notify decedent affairs," Walden said.

"Thanks, Meg," Collins replied. "Have we had any luck reaching any family members?"

"Not yet, doctor. They were sending someone out to the house to pick up Mr. Warren's mother. I told them you would like to have her brought in for an examination, and advised them to use full contact protection."

"Fine, Meg, let me know when she arrives. Doctor Frame and I are going to check on our other patients."

"Will do, doctor," she replied . "Oh, if you get a chance, we made a fresh pot of coffee."

"Just one pot?" he asked with a backward glance. "I hope it's a big one."

Chapter 3

Day 1

Home Of Doctor Laura Stewart,

Chief of Infectious Disease Control Unit

A light rain had been falling, and Laura Stewart closed the umbrella, shaking the water from it, as she and her husband Bill returned home from dinner. It was one of those rare occasions when they were both home long enough to enjoy an evening out "That was wonderful, Bill," she said, slipping off her wet coat and shoes at the door.

"Yes, it was, and we could do it more often," he answered, hanging her damp coat in the laundry room.

Fluffing out her hair she said, "Please, Bill, let's not go through this again. Can't we just once have a quiet night together that doesn't end in a fight about my job?" Turning away she walked down the hall to the living room.

Bill hung up his coat and followed her down the dark hallway. "All I'm saying, Laura, is that you're spending more and more time at the hospital or running off to some far-flung corner of the earth, tracking down some new and exotic disease. When are we going to have some time to spend with each other and do all those fun things that we used to talk about?"

Laura switched on the lamp beside the couch, then turned to look at him. The sight of his still-boyish face, even when it wore a frown, made it hard to get too mad at him. But she still didn't think she deserved the blame for this. "Bill, for God's sake, this is my job. It's what I want. I've spent close to ten years of my life to get where I am. You spend time on trips and seminars. You love your work, and I love mine." She sat down on the couch and reached for the remote control.

Bill put his hand on hers. "Laura, you know I spend most of my time in a classroom. My trips, as you call them, are an occasional overnighter up to the Blue Ridge or Wintergreen for my geology field work, not halfway around the world for a month or two at a time."

Laura sighed. "Bill, can we just forget it for tonight?" The beeping of her pager interrupted her. She took it out and glanced at the read-out. "It's the hospital," she said.

Settling into his large recliner, Bill said, "I rest my case. I see another quest starting."

He watched Laura and thought back to when they had first met. Her deep husky voice, full figure, and long shiny black hair had drawn him to her. They met during a field trip he had made to her native Spain. They'd dated and had wonderful times together. When they married, they had great hopes of long working vacations, but after five years, they knew they were growing apart.

Laura picked up the phone and punched in the number.

After a few short rings she heard:

"Emergency room, Walden, may I help you?"

"Yes, this is Doctor Stewart, someone there paged me."

"Oh yes. Doctor Collins has been trying to reach you. Hold, please, and I'll get him."

Laura shook her long hair off her shoulders and looked at Bill. She was about to answer his last remark when she heard Collins' voice.

"Laura, Wayne Collins here"

"Yes, what can I do for you, Wayne?" she asked.

"I hate to disturb you this time of night, but we have a situation developing here and I really could use your help."

"Of course I'll help, if I can. What's wrong?"

"Well, to tell the truth, I really don't know. At about seven o'clock tonight we started to receive patients presenting with convulsions, severe abdominal pains, nausea, diarrhea, rising temperatures, erratic respiration, and rapid heart beat. So far they've brought in eight patients, two of them coded, and we lost both of them."

"Oh boy! Do you have anything at all to go on?"

"Not yet. Doctor Bennett from neurology has also examined them but hasn't found anything conclusive, and no obvious organisms were seen in the microscopic exam."

"Okay, I'll get there as soon as I can."

"Thanks," he said. "Hopefully, by then some of the lab reports will be back. I'll give you an update when you get here."

Turning to Bill, she said, "I'm sorry. . ."

Bill snapped, "I know, Laura, it's an emergency, and you have to go again."

"Please, Bill, this sounds serious. I'll call you as soon as I can." Then, walking over to him, she kissed him and said, "We'll talk later."

"Yeah, later," he said, walking her to the door. "Be careful, you're not germ proof."

Smiling, she slipped into her damp shoes and coat, and then closed the door behind her. While she waited for the garage door to open, she pinned her long hair to the top of her head, then eased the car out into the misty night air. Thinking about the look on Bill's face when the pager went off, she realized they really hadn't done much together since their honeymoon in Hawaii five years ago. They really must do something new, and exciting.

She drove down highway 53 and headed toward the hospital. She glanced up as the headlights illuminated the road sign and read the all too familiar message, "Entering Albemarle County. Leaving Fluvanna County." Focusing again on the dark road in front of her, she cautiously made the tight turn past Ash Lawn Highland, the home of James Monroe, the fifth president, the originator of the Monroe Doctrine. The narrow, winding mountain road then wound up past Monticello (little mountain), Thomas Jefferson's home, one of the most frequently visited landmarks in the country, and one of the reasons why Virginia was known as the Mother of Presidents.

Past the entrance to Monticello, Laura continued slowly down the dark, rain-slicked road passing historic Michie Tavern and made a right turn onto the highway that would take her to the hospital.

Laura's thoughts switched back to the call from Collins. She knew he was not the sort to overreact. The urgency in his voice told her that whatever happened was truly worrying him.

Piedmont Medical Center, a complex of several buildings, had undergone considerable changes over the years. The facility contained six hundred beds, not including the nursery.

Besides the main hospital buildings, the complex included the Radiology Department, Oncology Lab, Surgical Operating Rooms, CU units, outpatient facilities, and emergency room. In addition there was a medical school, science building, and a school of nursing, all of which had access to a large medical library.

As Laura approached the hospital, she saw the flashing lights of an ambulance arriving at the emergency room. She   pulled around to the secured entrance at the rear of the hospital. The rain that had slowed to a mist had become heavy again. Pulling into an open spot she got out of the car, raised her umbrella, and hurried into the emergency room.

She noted the special quarantined area guarded by two of the hospital's security force. Not a good sign, she thought as she approached the desk.

"Where can I find Doctor Collins?"

"He's in conference room one. Shall I page him?" asked the young nurse seated behind a pile of charts.

"No, that's okay, I'll meet him there." Laura placed her wet coat over her arm and walked toward the conference room, located just off the emergency room. She paused a moment outside the door, then knocked and entered. Three men were seated around the conference table, Styrofoam coffee cups in front of them.

"Thank you for getting here so quickly," Collins said, looking up as she closed the door. "You know Andy Frame, Charlie

Bennett?"

"Yes, I do," she replied as they nodded to her. "Looks like you all have had a busy night."

"I'm afraid it's only beginning," Collins said, standing and picking up the cup of lukewarm coffee in front of him. "Care for a cup?" he said as she hung up her coat and umbrella.

"I sure would. It's real nasty out there tonight."

Collins sipped his coffee and said, "According to the news, a category three hurricane is moving slowly in from the Gulf of Mexico, with 130 mph winds. It is expected to come ashore along the Louisiana coast, and we'll probably feel the effects within seventy-two hours."

"I hope this isn't a precursor to what's to come," Frame said, handing Laura a cup of hot coffee.

"Bite your tongue, Andy. One problem at a time is quite enough, thank you," she said as she wrapped her hands around the cup and took a sip of the steaming coffee. She looked towards Collins and asked, "What's the situation?"

"Well," Collins said, sitting on the edge of the table, "as I told you on the phone, they began to come in about seven o'clock tonight. The first four have been the worst so far. One coded on the helicopter, and we continued to work on him here but we lost him. His wife turned bad about an hour later with the same results. Right after my call to you, six more patients arrived, bringing our count to ten within the last three hours, and all are presenting in the same manner."

"I think the count may have just gone up," said Laura. "Another unit pulled around back as I arrived."

Collins continued. "We have them all on IVs and we're giving broad spectrum antibiotics and acetaminophen suppositories. The spinal taps and EKGs on three of them are completed and they are running CT scans now. We were just about to go over what we know when you came in."

Bennett, picking up the papers in front of him said, "For starters, the spinal fluid in all three was clear. The pressure in each appeared to be normal, the highest being Mrs. Warren." At

Laura's inquisitive look, he said, "She was the second one we lost. The few results we have back so far show no signs of either bacterial or viral meningitis. We are even running India stains along with the antitoxin tests. It will be twenty-four to forty-eight hours before we get the rest of the culture results."

"Your opinion?" Doctor Stewart asked.

"If I had to guess, at this point I would say we could be dealing with some sort of toxin, but it's way too early to tell. All the blood work so far has come back negative. The white cells are high, which is consistent with a major infection. The red cell and platelets are normal. We're running all the usual tox screens and we should have some very preliminary results back from the tox lab in the morning."

"How do the vitals look?" Laura asked, looking up from the notes she had been taking.

"The blood pressures have been elevated for their respective age groups and apparent physical conditions. The respiration has been very erratic, between fourteen and thirty per minute, the worst of them again being Mrs. Warren. She ran from a high of thirty-four to a low of fourteen. Pulse and heart rate have been averaging 150 to 170. We've been administering digitalis, but so far it doesn't seem to have had much effect on slowing it down."

"Have they begun a post-mortem on Mr. Warren?" she asked.

"No," Collins replied. "We're still waiting to get authorization from his mother."

"Have you spoken to the medical director yet?" Laura asked.

"Oh yes! I've alerted Doctor Singleton. I also had Nurse Walden update the nursing supervisor and she's ready to implement the emergency plan if needed."

"When can I see these patients?"

"We can do that right now. Want to come along, Andy?"

"I'll be in the lab if you need me," Charlie said picking up his papers.

Chapter 4

Day 2

Piedmont Medical Center

John Singleton, medical director of Piedmont Medical Center, loved morning best of all. Today, though, was different; his mood was as gray as the weather. A fine mist covered the rain-soaked grass as he arrived at the hospital deeply concerned by Collins' call. He went directly to his office, pushed aside the messages his secretary had left there, and began making calls to set up the meeting he knew would be necessary. He assured everyone that their questions would be answered at the meeting. He knew that many of the questions they had were the same ones he was asking himself.

Collins arrived as he was finishing the last call. He looked like a man who had been up more than one night in a row. Singleton motioned him to a chair. "Tell me everything you know about the current situation."

Collins answered without preliminaries. "Five more patients died during the night, and several in critical condition are being treated in the isolation ward. We have full quarantine procedures in effect, and we have a command post set up at the nurses' station. We're going to have to give something to the media. They've been here most of the night looking for information."

"I see," Singleton said sitting back behind the desk. "Have you checked to see if any of the area hospitals are treating similar cases?"

"Yes, I have, but none have been reported. I've asked that such cases be diverted here."

"Good," Singleton sighed. "That should minimize the chance of wider exposure.

"As for the media, with all the traffic that's been on the scanners over the last several hours, they're sure to pick up on this situation."

Glancing at his watch, he continued, "It's 10:30 a.m. and I've called an 11:30 a.m. meeting with all of the department heads. I also invited members of the local press and law enforcement agencies. We need their assistance in controlling the speculation that usually occurs during events like this. Disseminating information is the media's job, but I won't condone any sensationalism. I have some other calls to make. I'll see you in the main conference room in an hour."

At 11:30 Singleton walked into the conference room and looked around at the small crowd gathered there. As he stepped up to the microphone, the noise in the room was reduced to a low murmur. "Can everyone hear me?" he asked, testing the sound system. At a nod from Andy Frame in the back of the room, Singleton began.

"I want to thank you, ladies and gentlemen, for coming this morning, especially on such short notice. We are faced with a situation that has developed over the past twenty or so hours, and is escalating. We are not even sure how to classify it. It does appear to be approaching epidemic proportions.

"As of 8:00 o'clock this morning we had seven deaths directly linked to this, for lack of a better word, disease. We have ten more patients in an isolation ward who are displaying the same symptoms, and they are in critical condition."

While he spoke the media listening intently, hastily scribbling notes.

"We have activated the emergency plan. Our nursing supervisor, Cheryl Mosby, will explain what this plan entails. Other members of the medical staff will follow her. Please hold your questions until each of them has spoken. We will answer them then." Turning, he said, "Ms. Mosby."

"Thank you, Doctor Singleton," she said, stepping forward from a group of white-clad medics. "I'm sure most of you are aware that all hospitals are required to have on hand a decisive plan to handle unexpected emergencies such as this. For those of you who may not be familiar with the procedure, I will try to give you a brief overview. The activation of such a plan immediately calls on the resources of all areas of hospital services, many of which are represented here this morning. They include medical staff, house keeping, social services, security, and legal, just to name a few. As Doctor Singleton stated, I initiated the emergency plan at the request of Doctor Collins. For the last several hours' personnel from all the areas mentioned and many others have been arriving at the hospital. All agencies involved were notified and we are now at full commitment. All precautions are being taken to ensure the safety of those directly involved in these tasks."

"Thank you, Ms. Mosby," said Doctor Singleton as he returned to the microphone. "I will now ask Doctor Wayne Collins, chief of emergency medicine, to give you a chronological description of what has occurred. Doctor Collins."

Collins rose from his chair and walked toward the microphone. He had managed to get about three hours of broken sleep. His eyes were red, his face was drawn, and he was functioning on the twelve cups of coffee he had had during the night. He hoped he looked better than he felt.

"Good morning," he said. "Last evening a Med-Flight helicopter brought in the first affected patient. That patient went into cardiac arrest during the transport. Resuscitation efforts were initiated en route and continued in house, regrettably without success. Shortly after the helicopter's arrival, two ambulances arrived with the wife and in-laws of the first gentleman. Within less then three hours, the wife expired. During the early morning hours the other family members, and four other people not related to the family, have succumbed to this illness. During this time, a medical team consisting of Doctor Bennett, chief resident of neurology, Doctor Stewart, chief of infectious disease control, several staff doctors and nurses, as well as myself have been working to identify and isolate the agent causing this disease. Doctor Stewart from IDC will tell you what steps are presently being taken. Doctor Stewart."

Laura rose to speak; she could feel the tension in the room. Her training had prepared her to cope with burgeoning new infectious diseases. She hoped that she could meet the expectations that the public would demand of her. There were many questions and concerns to be addressed and she prayed that she could at least help to keep the anxiety from becoming panic.

"Ladies and gentlemen, as my colleagues have indicated, we are dealing with a unique condition. I'll not attempt to minimize its seriousness. What we have witnessed in the past hours is testimony to the erratic and deadly effects that this 'disease,' using Doctor Singleton's word, can produce.

"What I do want to emphasize is that this is not the first, nor will it be the last time that we or some other facility will be faced with something this deadly. There are procedures and a vast array of modern equipment and knowledge available to us, much of which has already been deployed.

"The Centers for Disease Control in Atlanta were brought in this morning after conferring with the director of the Health Department. Patient blood and culture samples are already on their way to Atlanta for analyses, and they are prepared to send us a team if that is indicated. The purpose of these tests is to help us identify and isolate the nature and origin of this disease. I can assure you that we will use all the resources necessary to stop this epidemic. Now, ladies and gentlemen, we will try to answer some of your questions before we end this meeting. I'm sure you understand that time is crucial and we must make the most of it."

A portable microphone was moved through the room as hands rose to be recognized. A short, stocky man stood to be heard. "Tom Rigby from the Central Courier. I have a question for Doctor Stewart. Doctor, do we know anything at all about this illness?"

"Very little, Mr. Rigby. From the preliminary test results obtained, we feel that we are dealing with some form of powerful agent that can severely affect the body within hours, producing several rapid changes in the heart rate, respiration, and blood pressure as well as abdominal distress. As I said, we are hoping to get confirmation and identification from the CDC."

The microphone was moved to the center of the room, and Wade Jennings from the Dispatch spoke. "Doctor Collins, we have no information yet on the names of victims. Is there a reason for that?"

"Yes, there is, Mr. Jennings. Because of the short time in which these deaths have occurred, notification of the next of kin has not been completed, and we feel we owe that to the families."

"Is that the only reason, doctor, or is there more you're not telling us?"

"Nothing more at this time, Mr. Jennings, and I hope that you will keep speculation out of your report," Collins answered curtly.

A trim figure, with a tight crew cut stood at the side of the room with hand raised. "Sergeant Pickett, Police Department, Central Division. Doctor Singleton, sir, I will be coordinating traffic control and assistance requests with your security department. I would like to discuss the potential problem areas with you at the conclusion of this meeting."

"That will fine, sergeant. Please come to my office when we adjourn."

The questions continued until Singleton held up his hand and said, "Ladies and gentlemen, we really must get back to our patients. In closing I will emphasize that we are going to need everyone's help in this matter. We're counting on the media to be direct but accurate in reporting to the public to avoid any unnecessary panic. We will report any new developments to all of you as soon as they are available. Thank you again for your attendance, and hopefully the next time we meet we will have more positive news."

As the room emptied, Singleton turned to Collins and said, "Doctor, that hurricane might be another problem, as if we don't already have enough to deal with. Just before I came down to this meeting, I was notified that hurricane Flora is maintaining its strength and is projected to hit this area with, at the very least, a category one force."

"With all due respect sir, if we don't identify the source of this outbreak pretty damn fast the hurricane will be the least of our problems."

"I'm well aware of that, doctor. But this hospital has to be prepared for the worst, and if it's not, it's my reputation on the line."

"Frankly, sir, I don't have time to worry about your reputation. I have a ward full of dying patients who expect my team and me to help them and right now, we don't have a clue."

"Then you'd better get out of here and find some answers, doctor. In the meantime, I'll stay in contact with all the emergency coordinators from the surrounding counties and the Red Cross. Now, let's deal with the problem at hand."

Chapter 5

Day 2

Offices of Agrotex Research Laboratories

The week had not gone well for Doctor Tyler Wilson, head of the Research and Development division of Agrotex Laboratories. Agrotex, an independent facility engaged in the development and testing of specially treated strains of corn developed through genetic engineering, is located in the foothills of the scenic Blue Ridge Mountains. The Shenandoah Valley and Blue Ridge region cover most of western Virginia. Its outstanding feature is the Shenandoah Valley, a part of the Great Appalachian Valley.

It stretches for about 155 miles between the Alleghenies of West Virginia and the Blue Ridge. The rich soils of the valley make it one of the most fertile parts of the state. It produced a major portion of food for the South during the War between the States. It was a natural as well as a beautiful setting for a business serving the needs of modern industrialized agriculture.

The Agrotex laboratories, built in a park-like setting, was spread out over ten acres. The buildings were modern, with flat roofs and glass fronts. The grounds were kept immaculate by a team of gardeners working daily to keep the lawns and hedges trimmed. As fast as leaves fell from the trees, they were swept up and used as mulch for the flower gardens now in full bloom.

Genetic engineering had originated during the late sixties and early seventies, with experiments using viruses, bacteria, and small free-floating rings of deoxyribonucleic acid (DNA),

29

called plasmids, found in bacteria. The techniques of genetic engineering allow scientists to identify specific genes from an organism's chromosomes. They are then able to clone or make a large number of identical copies of that gene. After examining the copy in detail, they can modify it in some manner and reinsert it into the genetic material of the organism from which it came or the genetic material of a similar or very different organism.

Of all the food products that have been subjected to genetic engineering experiments, corn has enjoyed the greatest success. Recent work has shown progress in producing species of corn that have exhibited resistance to insecticides and displayed herbicide tolerance.

Agrotex used the principle of the splicing or recombining of RNA and DNA molecules to alter an existing species or strain to create a new one. It was felt that by treating hybrid feed, developed through this process, with special growth additives and hormones, healthier and more productive birds could be produced for the poultry industry. Testing of genetic engineering usually proceeds slowly when working with recombinant organisms, primarily because their final test must be done outdoors in test fields.

Wilson's trouble had started with the failure of an important test of a new feed product. After several weeks of testing, a recent experiment using a control group of chickens began to go bad. The birds became agitated, egg laying stopped, and within a couple of days some of the birds had died. Surprised by this event, the technicians had retained a sample of treated meal for analyses and further testing. The remainder was ordered sealed and removed to a holding area where it would be held pending the outcome of an investigation. If tests showed it to be contaminated in some way, it would be destroyed by incineration. The affected chickens were removed to the medical lab for thorough examination.

The birds had been fed genetically engineered grain treated with a sterile bacteria culture containing the genes producing thyroid stimulating hormone (TSH), as well as the growth hormone Somatotropin and antibiotics. The special bacillus strain they had engineered was one that contained a gene defect preventing it from developing spores. This would result in the death of the bacteria when they were sterilized before applying them to the grain. These hormones that support both growth and energy levels in human and nonhuman life would be deposited on the grain without any dangers from the bacteria that produced them. Even though earlier tests with growth hormones on poultry had not produced the results seen in cattle, Wilson felt that in the right combination, and introduced through a hybrid grain, these engineered bacteria could help develop larger and healthier poultry with a substantial increase in egg-laying ability. The lab results on the meal had shown no signs of contamination or foreign substances.

Wilson ordered a thorough post-mortem beginning with the skinning or defeathering of the birds. The first area examined was the head and neck. Then the head and muscles were inspected by incision to check for any disease condition. This was followed by a careful examination of the internal organs, known as a viscera's inspection, to further check for any signs of abnormality. Examinations of the external and internal carcass surfaces, including the air sacs, was also conducted, all with negative results.

The tests run on the birds showed an unusually large presence of the Campylobacter jejuni bacterium, normally considered a relatively harmless occupant of the gastrointestinal tract of both wild and domestic animals as well as poultry. The major concerns to Doctor Wilson and his staff were that, when compared to the bacteria found in birds not involved in testing, these bacteria appeared to have mutated into a more aggressive and resilient strain. More significant was that they appeared to be reproducing at an alarming rate.

Considering these developments, Wilson had ordered a complete review of the process and a thorough examination of this new form of Campylobacter jejuni bacteria. He was determined to isolate the cause of this event, and to discover if the problem lay with the treated grain or with the poultry, before any news of these test results were released.

He was aware that, although the concept of genetic engineering was widely known and used, in some quarters there was much concern as to its long-term effects. He remembered the public debate about the safety of recombinant organisms during the seventies. This resulted in government bodies being set up to monitor and screen experiments and the institutes conducting them, to ensure that appropriate safety guidelines were in place. He had always made sure that Agrotex conducted its work within these guidelines. Wilson had been with the company from the beginning. Its good name meant as much to him as his own. The president, Frank Sampson, had been leery of getting involved in genetic engineering, but Wilson had persuaded him. It wasn't just for profit, he had said. The president had laughed at that. He also had a background in biochemistry, and respected Wilson's ideas. Wilson's work had helped the company grow to what it was today, one of the largest corporations in this field.

What bothered Wilson most about the recent failure was less the embarrassment of poor results than the sloppiness it implied. He had always felt angry when he read of the tragedies brought about by industrial shortcuts or careless science. Now he was facing the possibility that a potentially grave mistake had been made, and on his watch. At least it had been caught at an experimental stage, before things had gotten out of control.

Just then his secretary buzzed him, and he picked up the phone. The call was from Jim Brown in the maintenance department. Brown told him that Bob Warren had been rushed to the emergency room last night, and died shortly after. The cause of death was still undetermined, but several others in his family had been ill as well. Maybe something they ate.

Wilson hung up the phone and turned in his chair to gaze solemnly out the large window. He watched the rain pour down the glass.

Warren had been with the company since it had opened five

years ago, as long as Wilson, and had worked his way up to a supervisor's position in the maintenance department. Wilson found it hard to believe that he had died so abruptly. He had spoken to Warren a few days earlier and recalled how excited he'd been about the vacation he and his wife were finally going to take, now that their small chicken farm was producing so well. He knew that the Warrens made extra money from the sale of the chickens and eggs to the residents in their small community. Must be that feed, he had said.

Wilson had not given it a second thought, and now he told himself that it was probably a coincidence. But at the same time he buzzed for his secretary.

"Yes, Dr. Wilson?"

"Get me maintenance," he said.

"Yes, sir." He was trying to sound calm, but he could tell by her voice that she knew something was wrong.

When Brown answered, he asked, "Do you remember who was involved in the removal and storage of the quarantined grain products from the Alpha test?"

"No, sir, but I'll check." Brown left the phone to inquire then came back. "Why, that is, was, Bob Warren, Dr. Wilson. Is there some problem we can help you with?"

"No, thanks," Wilson answered, "I think this is one for me to handle."

He was about to call Frank, and then caught himself. It should be the hospital first. The phone rang before he could pick it up. It was the state Health Department. They had questions about something they had found at the Warren farm.

Chapter 6

Day 2

Piedmont Medical Center

Emergency Room

Wayne Collins returned to the ER following the meeting. He knew that his heated exchange with Singleton, whose concerns were more political than clinical, would only add to the tension. His own encounter last evening with Wade Jennings didn't do much to ease the tensions in the ER. Jennings kept pushing for answers until he had him removed by security. Though the storm might cause added problems   his first priority was this epidemic. Sitting at his desk in the far corner of the ER he sipped on yet another cup of coffee and half-heartedly ate a sandwich. He reviewed the morning reports and noted that a total of twenty-five patients had been admitted and placed in isolation facilities. The one bright spot in the reports was that the heart rate of several of the patients finally had begun to stabilize.

He looked up as he heard Laura Stewart's voice. "Here you are," she said as she poured herself a cup of coffee and sat down. "Did you find anything new in those?" she asked nodding at the papers before him.

Looking down at the reports, he said, "Increasing the digitalis seems to have worked. We've also made some headway in slowing down the convulsions, but they're still dying." He tossed the reports on the table in frustration.

"Well, I have some news for you."

"Really?" Collins said getting up and pacing, as was his habit.

"I think we might have gotten a little closer to identifying whatever this is," Laura said.

"Go on."

"The Health Department and Extension people went out to the Warren farm and did a thorough inspection. When they checked the feed there, they found a canister of meal from Agrotex Laboratories."

"What does that give us?"

"Well, according to the Extension folks, Agrotex doesn't distribute to the public. They're strictly a research company."

Rubbing the tight muscles in the back of his neck he asked, "Do we know what kind of testing they were doing?"

"They don't have all the details yet, but they think it might involve genetic engineering of feed grain."

"Swell. We'd better find out what they were working with and how Warren got hold of it. On top of that what connection, if any, does it have with the rest of those affected?"

"The health and Extension people are on their way to Agrotex; we should know something soon. That's not all," she continued. "Social Services brought in Mr. Warren's mother, and I gave her a complete going over."

"And?" he asked.

"Wayne, she's fine. There's no sign of her being affected by whatever this is. Apart from a recurring intestinal problem brought on by an ulcer that flares up from time to time she's in remarkable shape for her age. I have a call in for her family doctor to see if there's anything else in her file that may be a factor."

"There has to be a reason for her not being affected along with the rest of the family. What about her medication, is she on any kind of antibiotic?"

"No, I thought of that too. The only thing she's on now is medication for her ulcer and high doses of antacids."

"We're missing something, Laura. It's probably right in front of our noses. We may have a bigger problem; it might be more than the feed that's responsible. Have we heard anything from the CDC in Atlanta?"

"No, it's too soon. The Health Department had chickens from the Warren farm sent to the Richmond lab for testing. They said that they'd send the results to the CDC as soon as they were available."

A staff nurse interrupted. "Doctor Collins, I'm glad you're here. We have a patient I think you should look at right away."

"What's the problem?"

"Her name is Kelly Ryman. She's twenty-three years old, and is expecting her first child in less than two weeks. She's also running a fever and is beginning to convulse. Her husband came in with her, and the poor guy is pleading with us to do something."

Collins snapped, "We're doing everything we can! Right now the best thing you can do is to keep these people calm." He looked at her worried face and thought of his own wife and kids. "I'm sorry about snapping like that," he said.

"I understand, doctor, it's just so frustrating. Some of them are so young and frightened."

"I know, and it never seems to get easier. Let's go see this young lady. Laura, I'd like you to come too, if you have the time."

"I'll make the time."

As they hurried to the room, Collins turned to the nurse. "You said the girl was affected. What about the husband?"

"No, sir, he's fine. They have him in quarantine as a precaution, but he shows no signs of distress."

Shaking his head, Collins turned to Laura. "We have to talk to him and see what he can tell us. Maybe he can shed some light on this."

"Agreed," she said, nodding thoughtfully. "This is the second time we've had close family members not affected, first Mr. Warren's mother, and now this young man."

When they entered the room Collins saw Walden going over the girl's chart. "Good to have you back on the line, Meg," he said as she handed him the chart.

"Thank you, doctor, a few hours' rest works wonders."

Laura looked at the girl lying on the examining table. She

was flushed, and the last convulsion had just ceased. Her swollen stomach and pale appearance made Laura shiver. She stepped close to the bed, taking Kelly's hot hand in her own. "Kelly, I'm Doctor Stewart, and this is Doctor Collins. We're here to help you. We also need your help. Do you understand?"

"Yes," Kelly replied in a voice that was just above a whisper. "How can I help? I thought it was just labor pains."

"Kelly," Laura continued, "can you tell us what you did and where you were in the last forty-eight hours?"

"Yes," she said, squeezing Laura's hand. "For the most part, I was at home."

"Did you eat out anywhere?"

"Only at the town fair. It's a family day get together that runs every year at this time."

"Kelly, did they serve chicken?"

"Why yes," she replied. "They have bacon and eggs, pancakes, and all sorts of chicken. They even have an egg-eating contest. Everyone enjoys watching that, but it makes me sick, especially now in my condition."

"Did you and your husband eat any of the eggs or chicken?"

"Bobby was mad because he loves barbecued chicken and he had to miss the fair because of work, so I went alone. I ate some eggs and bacon, but I was very uncomfortable and didn't stay long. We've both gone to this fair since we were kids."

For the next ten minutes Collins and Stewart examined and talked to the girl. When finished, they stepped outside the room.

"Wayne, I think we have our source," Laura said.

"If those eggs and chickens came from the Warren farm, and if they were fed some of that test feed from the Agrotex project, we may be dealing with a totally new substance, one that we know nothing about."

"Good Lord," he said. "I don't want to think what this could do if there's more of that grain out there."

"Wayne, I'll notify the Health Department, their people should be at Agrotex now. Then I'll call Atlanta and alert them to what we may have. Right now," she continued, "I'm concerned for Kelly and her unborn baby." Suddenly putting her hand to her head, Laura turned and faced the wall.

"Hey, are you okay?"

"Yeah, I'm okay," Laura replied. Then, hesitating, she turned and said, "No, I'm not okay. This really stinks, Wayne. All the experience and technology and here we are trying to save a mother and an unborn child and hoping we make the right decision."

"Look, Laura, this kind of thing is tough on everybody. None of us is perfect, we just do the best we can and hope it's good enough."

Taking a deep breath, Laura raised her hands in resignation and said, "You're right, of course, it's just so frustrating. I'm going to call her doctor and give him an update on her condition. If Kelly is up to it, he may recommend doing a C-section. Then we can continue to treat them separately. It may be the best chance of saving both of them. I'll also call Doctor Lane. As the on-call attending anesthesiologist she might have to make the call on this."

"Good idea," he said, nodding affirmatively. "I'll go talk to Kelly's husband and let him know what's going on."

Collins found Bob Ryman seated in the waiting area, staring blankly out the window. His shoulder-length dark hair was pushed behind his ears and his plaid shirt hung over his jeans. Pulling up a chair, Collins said, "Mr. Ryman, I'm Doctor Collins and we have to talk. Kelly is a very sick girl. We may have to give her medication that we can't give an infant, so treating them separately may be our best chance. We feel that the best way to help both of them would be to perform a C-section as soon as possible."

Ryman walked to the window and placed both hands on the cold glass. Tracing a trickle of water with his fingers, he asked. "What's wrong with her? She was fine this morning, and then she got real bad."

"We don't know yet, Bob. I can only tell you we'll do everything we can to help both of them, and every other person affected by this, to recover," he said quietly. "Right now, Bob, medication is our main concern. If it becomes necessary for us to administer large doses of drugs to Kelly, it would very likely have an adverse effect on the baby. If a C-section is possible, they'll both have a better chance. The choice will be yours and Kelly's."

Looking away, then back at Collins, Ryman asked, "Can I see her?"

"Sure, come with me. I'll let you talk to her for a few minutes." They continued to talk as they walked to Kelly's bed.

"I'll leave you two alone. I won't be far away if you need me."

"Thank you, doctor," Ryman said as he took Kelly's hand.

Chapter 7

Day 2

Offices of Agrotex Research Laboratories

Sitting in the conference room at Agrotex, Tyler Wilson listened intently to the report given by the Department of Health and the Extension people about their concerns that the critical medical situation might be directly connected to one of Agrotex's projects. He hoped they were wrong, that the events of the last twenty-four hours could be undone. Before the first investigators had arrived, he had known what to expect. He pulled the files and notes on the project as soon as he heard about the samples of grain found at the Warren farm. Wearily, he took the podium.

"Ladies and gentlemen," he began, "I don't know yet how or why it happened, but it does appear that rejected samples from the alpha tests on project twenty-one were not quarantined as ordered, and were removed without authorization from the laboratory. It also appears that the grain may have been fed to poultry at the Warren farm."

Wilson continued, "I have instructed that all our resources be made available to the Health Department and other agencies now involved in this incident. Our main objective will be to confirm the presence of the treated grain in the poultry involved, and to determine what could have possibly occurred, and if it contributed in any way to the observed reactions in those ingesting the poultry." Looking to the back of the room he noted a hand raised. "Yes, Mr. Sterling, you have some questions?"

"Yes, sir. First, how did a farmer get possession of this test grain? And the next is more of a request, doctor. What the Health Department needs as soon as possible is the type and purpose of the antigen and growth hormone used in the testing. Also, what reaction your people noted that prompted them to halt the tests and order the grain quarantined."

"To answer your first question," Wilson said, "the farmer is or was an employee in our maintenance department. On occasion, when there are samples of grain that are used only for comparison and not testing, we have customarily allowed the employees to take the surplus home. In this case all the surplus grain was ordered quarantined pending the outcome of our findings. Regrettably, Warren must have taken the wrong grain. All the other information pertinent to the project will be made available to you before you leave, and any other findings will be faxed to you."

"Thank you, sir, that will be a big help," Sterling said.

"One other thing I feel worth noting," said Wilson, "is that our original tests on the birds involved in the project indicated the presence of what appears to be a new strain of Campylobacter jejuni bacteria. As most of you know, this is a common bacteria often found in poultry. This strain seems to be much more aggressive and appeared to cause a more severe reaction in the test birds. I therefore feel that further examination in this area is imperative. I have instructed our lab to repeat the test using samples of the suspect grain and a new flock of chickens to see if we can recreate the same conditions in the birds and in the bacteria. We'll pass the results on to your people and to the CDC in Atlanta."

"There's one more thing I don't understand, which maybe you can clarify it, doctor," said Sterling.

"What's that, Mr. Sterling?"

"In reading this report on the alpha test, it indicates that two tests were run. The first, using the same grain, seemed to have gone according to your expectations. It was with the second test that you ran into problems."

"That's correct."

"What, then, sir, was the difference that caused the failure of the second test?"

"A good question, and one that we have asked ourselves. It's also why we're repeating both tests. The only difference, and it may prove to be a significant one, is that the first test was done with laboratory birds raised under sterile conditions. The second test used ordinary farm birds. We hope that at the completion of these new tests we'll have a satisfactory answer for you."

"Thank you," Sterling said. "We'll leave one of our people here to interact with yours, to insure that we don't duplicate testing and lose precious time."

"Fine," said Wilson. "If there are no further comments or questions, we can adjourn and try to resolve this situation."

Wilson left the meeting and returned to his office. Sitting at his desk he buzzed his secretary and said, "I don't want to be disturbed except on matters related to the Warren situation." Wilson poured over his work, determined to stay all night if necessary to find an answer to this enigma.

Chapter 8

Day 2

Piedmont Medical Center

Infectious Disease Lab

Laura Stewart sat at a small desk in the corner of the lab intently reviewing the latest chemical and bacteriological test results as well as the pathology reports done on several of the patients. It was quite clear now that all those involved in this were to varying degrees being affected in the same manner. A check with the fair officials confirmed their suspicions that the Warren farm had indeed supplied the food served. What perplexed her most was that, with the exception of the senior Mrs. Warren, all of them had become ill after ingesting a meal served at the fair. That the senior Mrs. Warren had not attended the fair, but had eaten the chicken also raised at the Warren Farm only created more questions. She wanted to know for sure how this agent was formed and the mechanism by which it worked.

Laura placed the papers on the desk, stood up, and stretched wearily. She walked over to the window that overlooked the busy street below and watched the large puddles of the rain that had continued all day.

Her attention was drawn to the small radio on the shelf. She listened as the announcer broadcast the latest update on the impending hurricane.

"The Hurricane Forecast Center has just issued a hurricane warning for South Carolina and parts of North Carolina. Hurricane winds at 125 per hour are expected to strike the low-lying areas of South Carolina in the next ten hours. Tropical force winds will extend two hundred miles from the center. Mandatory emergency evacuations have been ordered throughout the region. All residents in the Carolinas and Virginia are urged to stay tuned for further updates on this storm."

My God, it just keeps getting worse, Laura thought. First we have an epidemic and now a storm. What's next?

She went back over the events of the past several hours. The faces of the patients etched in fear, the apprehension of the families as they waited to hear about the condition of their loved ones. The most agonizing of all was the thought of Kelly Ryman and her baby. The C-section had been completed successfully and now they both lay in an intensive care unit struggling to hold onto life.

The rain beat heavily against the window as she thought about her last conversation with her husband and how often their lives seemed to be guided more by their work than their personal needs. She remembered the fun things they had done during the first year they were married, when they were almost as young as the Rymans. And she thought of how, lately, it all seemed to get pushed aside.

Her musings were as dismal as the weather. She was startled by the shrill ringing of the phone. She walked back to the desk and picked up the receiver. "IDC, Doctor Stewart.'

"Doctor Stewart, Ken Sterling with the Health Department."

"Yes, Ken, I hope you have some good news for us."

"Some good, some not so good, doctor. The good news is that more and more it does not appear that we are dealing with an airborne, or contact contaminant, so we should able to ease up on the quarantine."

"Oh, thank God," she said. "That will make things a little less complicated. What's the bad news?"

"Well, the reports and test results from Agrotex show the presence of a new or mutated strain of Campylobacter jejuni bacteria, which appears to have been developed as a result of exposure to the treated feed. They are rerunning the experiment to see if they can create the same conditions in a new group of chickens. This bacterium has been known to cause some minor distress in birds but nothing like what we're seeing here. We also ran some tests on samples of the chicken found in the refrigerator at the Warren farm.

"Good."

"It gets better. Warren worked in the Maintenance Department of Agrotex. The head of their R&D division, Tyler Wilson, told me this himself. Anyway, we compared these tests with the Agrotex results as well as those from the lab in Richmond. They all point to the feed as a possible catalyst for whatever happened."

"Good work, Ken, that explains a lot of things. Let me know if you come up with anything else. I'll let everyone here know what we have."

"I'll be in touch," Sterling promised.

As she hung up, she thought, at last we're making some headway. Once they knew exactly how this agent worked on the body they could concentrate on how to counter it She then placed a call to Doctor Singleton and brought him up to date. She also advised him that all staff and outside personnel involved would no longer require total isolation. Additional information would be made available as it was received.

Taking some notes and test results, she left the lab and headed for the emergency room. She glanced at her watch as she stepped into the elevator: 7:30 p.m. She watched the floor numbers change on the digital panel, then waited as the door opened with a slight shudder.

As she entered the area, she asked a staff nurse, "Have you seen Doctor Collins?"

"Yes," the nurse replied, "he and Doctor Bennett are in the cafeteria."

"Thank you," Laura said and got back on the elevator. Entering the cafeteria she saw Bennett and Collins seated at a corner table and walked towards them. "Is this a private party or can anyone come?" she asked.

Collins turned. "Laura, by all means join us. I hope you're the bearer of some good news."

"Yes, thank God. I thought a little stress relief might be in order."

"Amen to that," said Bennett. "I think we're all ready for shore leave."

Laura sat down across from Collins. "Well, gentlemen, the Health Department just advised me that this disease doesn't appear to be transmittable through contact nor do they believe it to be airborne. All indications are that a new or highly mutated form of a rather common bacteria found in poultry may have developed into a powerful new strain which may have brought about the conditions we have seen in the past two days." She went on to relate Sterling's findings.

"Well!" Collins exclaimed. "At least we know how and why the grain was at the Warren farm. Does Sterling have any idea what went wrong?"

"They feel that the experimental feed used by Agrotex in their tests may in some way have contributed to the rapid change in the Campylobacter jejuni bacteria. Ken said that they're repeating the test to see if it produces the same results. If tests run on the chickens show the same type of mutation in the bacteria, we may have our source."

"Laura, once we know what we have, how long do you think it'll take the CDC to correlate the information and make some suggestions on how to neutralize it?" Bennett asked nervously.

"I'm not sure, Charlie, a lot will depend on just how different this strain of bacteria is and just how it works," she replied. "I called Dr. Singleton and briefed him."

"By all means, keep him happy," said Collins. "With everything we have going on, the last thing we need is another lecture on policy."

"I agree," Laura said. "Wayne, what's it looks like in the ER? Are there any new cases?"

"No, Laura, and thank God for that. I'm afraid we may lose

a few more before this is over, but right now we're just holding our own. I hope Atlanta has something on the shelf for this thing. We may not have time to start from scratch."

"It will be tomorrow at the earliest before we can expect to hear anything new," she said.

As they left the cafeteria she asked Collins. "Have you heard the latest weather forecast? It looks as if we may get hit pretty hard."

"I've been keeping up with the reports and it scares the hell out of me. The last thing we need is another complication. I shudder to think what this place could look like if this storm hits in the next couple of days. With all the additional trauma coming through here, we're going to be swamped."

"I hope I can get home before the rain gets worse," she said. "I'd better call Bill and let him know I still have a few people to see before I can leave."

Chapter 9

Day 2

Piedmont Medical Center

Staff Conference Room

Laura had filled Singleton in on the information concerning the possible presence of a new and deadly bacterium. He hastily called a meeting of all the department heads. A large flip chart had been brought into the room. On it was a step-by-step account of all that had occurred since the arrival of the first patient.

Singleton entered the room, and the din of voices gradually softened until the room was quiet and all eyes focused on the chart.

Singleton began. "I know all of you are deeply involved in attempting to identify and contain this event. Considering the new information now available to us, I feel a review of where we are is called for at this time. I will ask Doctor Stewart to share this information with you. Doctor Stewart."

Moving up to the front of the room, Laura pointed to the flip chart. "Most of you have followed the progress of this event since its onset. As you can see, the chart highlights the major areas of development. Earlier this evening I received word from the Health Department that we may be dealing with a powerful new strain of bacteria. The good news is that it does not appear to be airborne or spread by contact. The bad news is that it seems rapidly to attack multiple body systems and, in a sense, causes them to overload. This results in the violent conditions we have all observed.

"Pathology reports on most of the early arrivals indicate multiple perforations throughout the intestinal tract, most likely caused by the massive infection present in the late stages of this condition. It appears that the bacteria produce a proteolytic that literally dissolves the bowel. This action also appears to produce microscopic ulcers in a matter of minutes or hours instead of weeks or months. Doctor Hogan's examination did not indicate the presence of any necrotic areas or infarcts, though in some cases the infection appears to have spread to the heart valves and other organs causing a deadly systemic disease. Tissue samples were also taken from the cerebral cortex and sent to the toxicology lab to be tested for the presence of any exotoxins or endotoxins that might be associated with the bacteria. Large doses of clindamycin, erythromycin, and vancomycin do not appear to affect it significantly.

"It does appear that in all cases the substance was ingested through food, and we believe the host to be chickens or eggs that were served at a town fair. The Health Department discovered some containers of test feed that was given to the chickens on the farm that provided food for the affair.

"Right now the DOH and the Extension people are at Agrotex looking for answers. Chickens and eggs recovered from the farm have been sent to Richmond and the CDC for additional testing. As more information becomes available, we will pass it on to you." She returned to her seat, and Doctor Singleton stepped to the front of the room.

"Please remember," he said, "it is essential that we maintain our professionalism during this event. The public, the press, and the patients are all concerned and in many cases frightened by the violent manner in which this has affected their lives. Press releases will be issued as necessary.

"Thank you for your time and efforts, and I ask only that you deal in facts and reassure your families when talking to them that we are in control. If the community begins to panic, people are going to get hurt and our hospitals will be overwhelmed."

With the scraping of chairs, the medical staff filed from the room. Laura turned to Collins and said, "Wayne, I'm going to check with Doctor Lane. I'm really worried about the Ryman girl. I want to see how she and the baby are doing."

"Fine, Laura, let me know how they are."

As Collins walked away, his thoughts went back to the time he had spent in the Mideast during Desert Storm. They worried about what they might run across there in the way of germ warfare or disease. They were prepared for the worst, but they felt sure there was nothing that they couldn't treat. Now he knew they still had so much to learn. Approaching the isolation ward, he stopped and peered through the glass doors, looking at the line of beds and the faces of the patients lying in them. It was always the same. The faces were different, but the look of anxiety and confusion was always there.

Walking down the hall, he saw Doctors Bennett and Frame talking quietly in the corner. "Your thoughts, gentlemen?" Collins asked as he approached.

"Well, if it's a new viral or bacterial strain, I sure the hell hope they're right about it not being contractible by contact with the patients or by some airborne process," Bennett said irritably. "What really concerns me is, if this infection gets to the brain, finding an antibiotic that can get past the blood-brain barrier could prove difficult. I'm not going to feel better until we know for sure." And he walked away abruptly.

"What's eating him? I've never seen him lose it before," Frame said.

"He's been under a lot of stress these past few months, Andy."

"Well, let me tell you, this is one experience I won't forget. I guess this is what they meant when they said there are some things you just don't learn in medical school."

"Amen to that," Collins agreed. "You know, what really gets me is Warren's mother."

"Yeah, she's sort of the square peg in the round hole," Frame said, with a perplexed look on his face. "She still shows no sign of being affected, and we know that she ate the same meal, including the chicken, as the rest of the family. Finding out why might answer a lot of questions. I hope we'll be getting some information from the Health Department and the CDC soon."

"I would think so, Andy. Laura asked them to contact her the minute they get some answers from Agrotex." Looking at the clock on the wall, he said, "I'd better get to the unit. Hopefully we can hold our own till then."

He walked into the ER to find Bennett waiting. "Charlie, we have to talk."

"About what?"

"You know what. Your nerves, plus your mind isn't completely on your work. I know these past few months have been rough on you and Amanda; but damn it all, Charlie, right now you need to be concentrating on what's going on here. If you need help, talk to me."

"I'm sorry I've been so short-tempered, Wayne. Amanda having a baby this late in our lives is taking its toll. She had such a bad time with the twins she's really upset. This epidemic and not knowing what's going to happen is weighing heavily on her. I keep reassuring her but right now it's hard to convince her that everything will be okay. We'll both be glad when this is over."

"I understand, Charlie, and if you think it'll help I'll have Kate call her."

"She'd really appreciate that. She likes Kate and maybe it will help to talk to another woman. Thanks again, Wayne. Now I'd better get back to the lab. Call when you hear from the CDC."

"Sure, Charlie, the minute I hear."

Chapter 10

Day 2

Piedmont Medical Center

Emergency Area

Laura walked to the elevator and pushed the up button. While she waited her name was called over the intercom.

"Doctor Stewart, you have a call on line four." Stopping at the ER desk, she picked up the receiver of the phone that hung on the wall. "Doctor Stewart."

"Laura, it's Bill. I tried calling home and got no answer. I was worried. I've been listening to the newscasts. What's going on, hon? Are you okay?"

"I'm fine, Bill, just a little tired, everyone is. I should have called you sooner, but it's been crazy here. It's just so frightening to realize how quickly something like this can happen."

"Are you making any headway?"

"Some. We think we may be close to identifying the source but there're still a lot of unanswered questions. We haven't received any new cases in the past few hours, but my heart jumps every time I hear an ambulance siren."

"Look, Laura, I wanted to let you know just in case you got a chance to go home. I'm at the camp near Wintergreen. I want to survey a couple of spots for some geological trips and I figured this was as good a time as any. I'll call you when I get back."

Laura laughed. She had been afraid that Bill would be worried about her driving home in a rainstorm, and here he was, camping out in the middle of it. "Bill, do you think that's the best place to be, with a hurricane moving our way?"

"I'll be back long before that hits," Bill said.

"Bill, be serious, no rocks are worth that kind of risk. I hope you're not angry about anything I said last night." She had said that she had her work, and he had his. Was he trying to prove her right, by letting her come home tonight to an empty house?

"All forgotten. You know there're just times when it gets to be too much for me, missing your beautiful face. I hope I'll be seeing it again tomorrow night?"

Laura smiled. "Of course, Bill. But if you insist on looking for rocks in this weather, please, be careful."

"Same goes for bugs, Laura. You be careful, too."

She replaced the receiver then glanced at her watch, which said 11:00 P.M. She was in worse shape than she thought, she reflected, looking in a mirror. Composing herself she again started for the elevator. Reaching the outer doors, she saw Collins and Singleton talking to the hospital security chief.

Approaching them, she heard Singleton ask, "How bad is it, Fletcher?"

"It's not good, sir, and it's getting worse. The lobby is full of family, friends, and media, and they're all looking for answers, and quite frankly, sir, I don't know what to tell them. They're just plain scared. We're having a problem keeping the ER entrance clear for the normal arrivals."

"Fletcher, you're going to have to keep it together down there for a little while longer. Notify the county that you're going to need some backup. We must keep the entrances open to emergency vehicles and personnel."

"Yes, sir, I'll get right on it," replied Fletcher hurriedly leaving the area.

"I was hoping it wouldn't come to this," Laura said as she stood next to Collins.

"I'm afraid it's going to get worse and it doesn't look good for the hospital. Doctor, I want to know as soon as you hear anything from Atlanta." Singleton said and left the lobby.

"Mr. Charming," Collins said glancing at Laura. "I'm going to make a check of the ER before I leave."

"Okay, I'll see you in the morning. I still want to look in on the Ryman girl and her baby before I leave. Last time I checked they were just about holding their own. They tell me her husband has called eight times already. I'd like to be able to give him some good news."

Collins just smiled and walked back towards the ER. He couldn't help wondering how much longer this would go on. With every hour that passed the chances of losing more lives became greater.

Entering the waiting area he paused and looked around. He saw a middle aged woman talking quietly to some small children as she wiped tears from her eyes. At the far end of the room, he watched as an elderly man waving his arms wildly, vented his frustrations on a security guard. Collins moved on and wondered how much worse it would get.

The emergency room shift was changing, and Collins greeted the incoming staff. He began to confer with Doctor Ken Fraser, briefing him on the events of the past twelve hours.

While they spoke the ER doors swung open, and three stretchers were rolled in and placed in treatment rooms.

"What do we have here?" Fraser asked.

"We have a domestic that got a little out of hand, doc," the medic replied. "You got one female and two males with stab wounds." Fraser and Collins quickly evaluated each patient. The most seriously injured was a twenty-five year old male with a severe wound to the chest.Fraser turned to a staff nurse. "Let's get this one to the OR stat. We can take care of these two; all they need is some needle work."

"Right, doctor, I'll see to it right away," she replied.

Collins and Fraser each took a patient. They cleaned and stitched their minor cuts and bruises and released them. Pulling the rubber gloves from his hands, Collins dropped them into the medical waste container. Running his hand through his hair, he turned to Fraser and said, "I'm out of here, Ken, before you get more of the same. See you tomorrow."

Chapter 11

Day 3

Home of Dr. Wayne Collins

Driving home Collins went over in his mind the events of the past two days and wondered if they had missed something right under their noses. His mind wandered from the patients to his family. He'd called Kate and told her he would be home for at least a couple of hours. It was a short ride from the hospital to the house, and he was pulling into his garage before he knew it. Kate was waiting up for him and met him at the door. "Hi, honey!" he said, putting his arms around her and inhaling the soft musk aroma that she always wore. "You smell good," he whispered in her ear.

She smiled and said, "Sorry I can't say the same for you. Into the shower with you while I make something to eat."

Kissing her on the head, he walked upstairs to the master bedroom. It sure was good to be home. He removed his soiled clothes, dropped them on the floor, and stepped into the shower. Making the water as hot as he could stand it, he grabbed the soap and worked it into a good lather. With the pulsating spray of the shower hitting him, he felt the strain of the past two days slowly fade away. Reaching for his razor he carefully shaved his scruffy face. Fifteen minutes later he turned off the water and dried himself with a thick towel. Stepping back into the bedroom he pulled on a jogging suit and left the room.

Before going downstairs he looked in on each of his three children. Alexander, the oldest at nine, was looking more and more like him, he noted. Collins took the baseball and the bat off the bed and placed them on the night table. He was pitching this year for his little league team and was actually very good. He was growing like a weed and was all legs and arms.

In the bed next to Alexander lay Danny. At five, he was all boy. Every day he was going into a different profession when he grew up, and his side of the room reflected the changes. There was a toy doctor's bag with stethoscope hanging over the side. This was for the days he wanted to be like dad. Then of course there were his trucks, his rock collection, and his airplanes. While he looked at his youngest son, the boy turned over and kicked the covers loose. Bending over, Collins kissed him on the head and straightened the covers.

Leaving the boys room he went to check on Katlin. She was the mirror image of her mother, with the same auburn hair and small oval face. After taking dancing lessons for six months she was sure one day she would be a great ballerina. She had told her father that boys were stupid, which of course was fine with him. Her green eyes, closed now in sleep, could be most beguiling. He didn't want to think about the hearts she would break in the not-too-distant future. He tucked the blanket about her and walked from the room.

"Please God," he whispered, "keep them all safe and healthy."

He turned and walked back downstairs to the kitchen where Kate was waiting, with an omelet and coffee. What a woman!

"You're looking much better, Doctor Collins."

"Yeah, and I feel a lot better too," he said sitting down at the table. "I'll feel even better after I eat some of this real food."

"Well, I'm glad you're home," said Kate. "You needed a break from that two-day stretch. Did you look in on the kids?"

"Sure did. Tell me, Kate, how do they grow so much in just a couple of days? I do miss all of you when I'm away like this."

"We miss you too. This thing at the hospital will get better and your schedule will be back to normal soon, won't it?" Kate asked, sitting close to him.

"It's not just this outbreak, Kate. Singleton is making noises again about procedural revues, scheduling, and training. I can handle the medical end of it but I get so damn tired of the politics." Taking a sip of coffee, he draped his arm about her and sighed.

"I know you have a lot on your mind, Wayne, but I'm worried about this storm. This might sound selfish, but I'd really feel a lot better with you home if it strikes. You know how frightened Katlin gets in thunderstorms."

" I'll do my best. But I can't promise to be home when it arrives," he said, shaking his head slowly. "It'll depend on the situation at the hospital."

Looking at him she saw the tired, worried look on his face.

"Kate," he said. "There's something I'd like you do for me."

"What is it?"

"I talked with Charlie today. Amanda is having a tough time with this pregnancy. It has both of them stressed out and it's beginning to affect Charlie's concentration. Would you give her a call and see if you can ease her mind?"

"I'll call her in the morning and see what I can do."

"Thanks, I know it'll make Charlie feel better."

Getting to her feet she cleared the table, while he went and sat in his favorite chair. He watched the late news and weather report. All and all the coverage of the emergency wasn't bad. No one was panicking, at least not yet.

"Okay, Collins," Kate said entering the room, "it's time for you to get a good night's sleep."

"I couldn't agree with you more," he said as they walked arm in arm upstairs to the bedroom.

The sirens kept getting louder, and he wondered why they weren't stopping. The sound penetrated his sleep-fogged brain, and he sat up with a start. The phone rang again, and he reached for the receiver.

"Collins here," he said sleepily.

"Doctor Collins, this is Meg Walden. I'm sorry to wake you but I thought you would want to know, we may have three more cases on the way into the unit."

He glanced at the clock radio on the night table, it was 5:30

A.M. "I'll be there as soon as I can, Meg. Thanks."

Kate sat up in bed as he replaced the receiver. "What's the matter, Wayne?"

"Sorry the phone woke you. It was the hospital. They think they may have three more cases. I have to go. You go back to sleep. I'll call you later." After a quick shower and shave, he leaned over and kissed her. "Kiss the kids for me," he said as he left the room and headed for the garage.

Chapter 12

Day 3

Piedmont Medical Center Isolation Ward

Laura Stewart had arrived early and gone straight to the isolation unit to check on Kelly Ryman. As she approached the bed, she could feel every nerve in her body tense. She had to get hold of herself. Last night before leaving, she had visited Kelly and found her asleep. Even though this was to be expected, she felt uneasy watching the young girl. She had witnessed the effects of some of the most devastating viruses and diseases in the world. Yet the thought of this young girl and her child struggling to hold on to life had affected her in a way that she had not experienced before. Maybe it was because the last couple of days she had been feeling that something in her own marriage was in danger of being lost, just as the Rymans were in danger of being lost to each other. She was determined to do everything in her power to help them win their battle. Standing next to the bed, she reached out and placed her hand on the girl's head. "It's Doctor Stewart. Can you hear me, Kelly?" she asked softly.

At first there was no response. Then Kelly slowly opened her eyes. She managed a weak smile, then reached for Laura's hand and held it close to her.

"How is my baby?" she asked in a whisper. "I miss her so much, and I've only seen her once."

"She's fine, Kelly." She was glad that she had been to the nursery to check on the newborn. "How are you doing?"

"I don't know. I'm afraid. I just want to go home and see Bobby and the baby again."

"You will, Kelly, I promise you will."

Still frightened by her ordeal, Kelly sighed and looked away. "Try and get some rest," Laura said. "I'll check on you later." She squeezed her hand and watched as Kelly drifted off to sleep.

Leaving the ward, she stopped at the nurse's station. "Nurse, if there's any change in Kelly Ryman's condition page me, please, and keep paging until you reach me."

"Yes, doctor," the nurse acknowledged.

Laura glanced back at the ward, and then walked to the elevator. She had to get back to the lab. There must be something else they could do.

Chapter 13

Day 3

Home of Charlie Bennett

Amanda Bennett woke and looked across the king-size bed at Charlie. She came up on her elbow and watched him as he slept. He had spent the last two days at the hospital and needed this rest. Lying back on her pillow, she closed her eyes and sighed. She could hear the rain pelting the windowpanes, good weather for staying in bed. She had a few minutes at least before the twins would be up and eating breakfast.

She loved the boys dearly and remembered all the anguish and pain she had undergone having them. Rubbing her hand over her large abdomen, she prayed she wasn't in for the same ordeal again.

The night the twins were born had been cold and rainy. She and Charlie had raced to the tiny hospital, where she had gone straight into labor and delivery. By the time the twins were born many hours later, she was completely exhausted and poor Charlie was a wreck.

This time she had chosen the best obstetrician she could find, and she had assured Amanda a smooth delivery. Still, a woman in her condition always felt a little uneasy after giving birth under less then perfect circumstances.

It had taken her months to get back on her feet after the birth of the twins. One baby would have been a handful, but two were a challenge.

It was a good thing her mother had been willing to help out. Amanda recalled all the time her mother had given to help bathe and feed the twins while she rested and regained her strength.

There were times she thought she would never get through the first month, let alone the first year now the boys were ten and she was starting all over again.

A girl would be nice this time. She smiled, as the baby kicked and moved about. She could have learned the sex of her unborn child when the sonogram was done, but she wanted to be surprised, and Charlie went along with her.

Their sitting room across the hall had been transformed into a nursery. The walls had been painted bright yellow, and the border of woodland animals with its sea foam green background would delight any child. The breeze moved the white organdy curtains at the window and stirred the mobile of baby animals hung above the crib. Though the baby wasn't due for two weeks, she and Charlie wanted everything ready. Even the twins had helped decorate the room.

Amanda came out of her reverie as the alarm sounded. Sitting up in bed, she reached for her robe and walked into the bathroom. Returning, she saw that Charlie had turned over but was still sleeping soundly. Tom and Steve were up and having cereal by the time she got downstairs. She started the coffee. Then, as she began to pour the juice, she hesitated. Placing her hand beneath her stomach, she said, "Ooh! That hurts," and sat down slowly.

"Looks like I may have you to keep me busy sooner then I thought, little one," she said, continuing to massage her stomach.

The rain continued to beat against the French doors that opened on to a deck off the bedroom. Bennett awoke to the voice of a newscaster recapping the events of the past evening. He wearily stretched and headed for the shower. He felt he could sleep for a week. He turned the water on high, and closed his eyes. Twenty minutes later he walked downstairs and into the kitchen, where Amanda and the twins were finishing breakfast.

"You're all up early," he said, sitting down at the table. As Charlie spoke, Amanda poured a cup of coffee.

"That smells delicious," he said as the hot steam rose from the cup.

"Hungry?" she asked.

"I'm starved, but I don't have time. I'll just have this coffee and some toast. Those last test results should be in, and depending on what they show, all hell could break loose."

Amanda sat next to him and took his hand. "Is it that bad, Charlie?"

Seeing the concern in her face he squeezed her hand and said, "I know you're on edge with this pregnancy and all that's happening at the hospital, but Doctor Kelsey told us that you and the baby are in fine shape, so try to relax." He remembered all too well the rough time she had had when the twins were born. The surprise they received eight-and-a half months ago, when they found out she was pregnant after ten years, had taken a lot of adjusting. So far everything was fine, but as he looked at her swollen feet and now very enlarged stomach he could see the discomfort she was feeling.

"Don't worry. I'll be all right," she said standing and arching her aching back. "The baby is very active this morning. Maybe all this rain is making him or her impatient to be on the move. Just like the father," she added with a smile. Bennett moved closer and placed his hands on her abdomen just as the baby gave a kick.

"That was a good one," she said.

He held her close. "It'll all be over soon, and we'll have another healthy child. It looks like this storm is going to be with us awhile, so you and the boys can spend a nice quiet day together."

"Yes, doctor," she said with a smile.

They walked to the front door, followed by the twins. He put on his raincoat, bent down, and hugged them both. "You take good care of your mother, and you," he said looking at Amanda, "if you need me for anything don't hesitate to call."

"I will," she said.

Chapter 14

Day 3

Piedmont Medical Center

Collins pulled into the doctors' parking lot alongside the emergency room, his mind full of questions. If these new cases were connected to the current epidemic, he thought, then there was no telling how many more they might get. He parked the car and ran through the rain to the emergency entrance, where Meg Walden met him.

"What's the situation?" he asked as he removed his dripping jacket and replaced it with a white coat.

"Three more new patients. Doctor Fraser is examining them now. They only arrived a couple of minutes ago. He's in room one."

"Fine, I'll join him there."

He entered the room and saw that Fraser was just completing the examination of one of the new arrivals. Putting on a pair of sterile gloves, and pulling Ken aside, he asked, "Well, Ken, what do you think? More of the same?"

"I haven't seen any test results yet, but on the surface I'd say there was a damn good chance."

"What do we know about them?"

"So far just what we were able to get from the ambulance crew. They come from the same area as the others. What we don't know is whether or not they were at the town fair and, if so, why it took this long to affect them."

Thanks, Ken, I'll have them moved to the isolation unit. Then I'll talk to Laura and bring her up to date on these new cases and see if she or Atlanta have any new ideas."

"I guess it's times like this that make us find out how good we really are," said Fraser.

"You have that right, Ken. Right now I'd be happy to know if it's the bacteria or some toxin it has produced that's causing this. A toxin could be worse than the bacteria itself, and a hell of a lot harder to treat."

Removing their gloves and tossing them into the waste bin both men left the room and walked back to the receiving desk. Fraser continued to brief Collins on the condition of the three new patients. They were all presenting with the same symptoms as those affected earlier but with less severity. The results of the tox screens, cultures and blood work were needed to confirm these as new cases of the resistant C. jejuni bacteria.

As they spoke, Fraser signed off on the patients' reports and put on his jacket. Turning back to Collins he said, "I'm going home to get a few hours sleep. If something breaks on this and you need a hand, just ring. I'll get in as soon as I can."

"You'll be the first on my list, Ken." Walking around the desk and sitting down, Collins called to Meg Walden who was restocking a med-cart. "How do we look for personnel this shift, Meg?"

"No problem," she said. "We're at full staff. I thought the storm might keep some of those who live over the mountain home, but we're okay."

"Good. I don't know how much worse this will get, but I don't want to be caught shorthanded at this stage of the game."

"Understood," she replied. Looking down at her check-off list, she seemed to have something on her mind.

"Anything else I should know about?" Collins asked.

Walden shook her head. "Nothing, doctor," she said, with a brief but reassuring smile.

Collins reached for the phone and dialed the IDC lab. After a few rings he heard, "IDC, Conway."

"Conway, this is Doctor Collins. Is Doctor Stewart in yet?"

"Yes, doctor, she's just coming through the door. It's Doctor Collins for you," he said, passing her the receiver.

"Good morning, Wayne. How are things in the emergency room?"

"I've had better days," admitted Collins. "Three more possible cases were brought in a short while ago. They're on their way to the unit, and we're waiting for the test results. Have you heard anything new from Atlanta?"

"Not so far. I was just about to recheck some of my notes, then call them. Let me know if these new cases are confirmed so I can pass that on, and I'll let you know the minute I hear anything."

"I hope it's soon, Laura."

"Me too," she said, replacing the receiver.

He turned back to Walden. "If Doctor Stewart calls, come and get me, no matter what I'm doing, okay?"

Meg nodded and watched him turn back to his work. She understood the urgency of the situation, and admired the way Collins kept focused on the matter at hand. She tried to do the same, and thought she was successful at it. But it was an effort, especially on a day like today.

As she walked to her car this morning, the wind was so strong it almost turned her umbrella inside out. She could not help thinking of Michael, and the storm that had taken him away from her. He was the first and so far the only man she had ever loved. They had met when she was a nursing student and he was in law school. Michael had been of medium height with sandy brown hair and clear hazel eyes. Meg tried to shake the images away because the thoughts of Michael were too painful. They had planned to be married, and everything seemed perfect. Then there had been a terrible thunderstorm. Michael had been cramming for exams. His mind must have been on his work, because the police said it appeared as if he never saw the eighteen-wheeler that hit him broadside. The sight of his broken body lying in the morgue played over and over again in her mind.

After graduating from high school, she had planned to pursue a teaching career, until her father had suffered a heart attack. She had called for an ambulance and made her own frantic

71

efforts to administer CPR. After her father's recovery, she decided to change her vocation to health care, determined to repay the debt for her father's life. People said she was all business. Her professional manner had a calming affect on the patients; she was considered one of the most capable nurses in the unit. Her thoughts were broken as the emergency room door opened again, and two medics appeared, rolling in a patient on a Gurney.

Chapter 15

Day 3

Piedmont Medical Center

Emergency Room

Collins finished signing off on the charts of the new patients and thought that whatever was causing this was certainly not selective in its actions. Sorting through each of the reports he noted the differences between them. There were two males, one a farmer in his early seventies, the other an auto mechanic in his twenties. The third patient was a forty-five-year-old woman, employed by the federal government. The only common link might be their attendance at the county fair. He thought he would do a little digging, and see what else he could come up with, as Andy Frame approach ed the desk.

"Wayne, I think you'd better take a look at the guy in room three. We were getting ready to move him to the unit when he began to convulse. I've stabilized him, but his vital signs are still borderline."

"Okay, let's take another look at him."

He entered the room. "This is Mr. Fong, a forty-year- old male. His respiration is irregular, and his blood pressure is elevated. Like all the others, he has a rapid heart rate. His stomach is distended, there is an absence of bowel sounds, and I think you'll find his chart interesting."

Looking at the chart, Collins studied the entries that had been made since the patient had been admitted. "I see what you mean, Andy. According to his wife, this man was fine this morning, then suddenly began to complain of severe pains and became feverish. When asked, she confirmed that they were at the fair.

"That could mean we have another problem. This thing may have an extended incubation period, and if so, we'd better keep a close eye on Mrs. Fong."

Turning to the nurse, he said, "Continue to monitor his vital signs and let me know immediately if there's any change."

"Yes, doctor." she said.

Leaving the room, he shook his head. "Damn it, Andy, we'd better nail this thing pretty soon or it could get ugly in here. I'd better call Laura. I told her Id let her know if there was any change in these new cases."

"I'm headed in that direction now," Andy said. "I can stop in and update her if you like. I've never been up there while anything this big was going on. It might be an education."

"Works for me. It'll give me a chance to do a little research of my own."

Frame headed for the IDC lab. Upon entering, he paused for a moment and studied the vast array of equipment that filled the room. Seated behind several tables that held test tubes and microscopes were white-coated lab technicians, each engrossed with the various tests they were running.

To his left was a large refrigerator used to store the many samples and cultures waiting to be tested. Hanging on the wall next to the refrigerator was a poster that read, "Research Saves Lives." The picture on the poster showed cancer survivors of all ages. Amen to that, thought Frame. Again glancing to his right, he saw Laura seated at a large microscope.

"Very impressive," he said as he approached her.

"Oh, Andy, you startled me," she said, looking up.

"So this is where you spend all your time."

"Yeah, this is my think tank."

"Have you found anything?" he asked.

"This strain of bacteria is amazing. I see it, but I still can't believe the rate at which it's dividing," Laura replied. "How about you, any progress with the new cases?"

"That's why I'm here. Wayne and I just left one of the new

arrivals, and he's reacting the same as the others. He just started convulsing. Fortunately we were able to stabilize him with meds."

"Hmm, interesting" she mused. "Although it adds to the theory that this thing may have a long incubation period."

"Yeah, Wayne just said the same thing. We feel like we're fighting with one hand tied behind our backs," Andy said, shaking his head.

"I know the frustration you're feeling, Andy. Sometimes it seems like the more answers we get, the more questions we have."

"What's taking so long?" he asked throwing up his hands. "They've dealt with this sort of thing for years. I don't understand why they can't get a handle on it."

Laura nodded. "Andy, the identification of new bacteria is often very difficult, especially one that has developed in such a short time and changed so abruptly. It takes several steps to put the puzzle together. First, microscopic observations are made to determine the size, shape, and appearance of the specimen after it has been stained. Then observations are made of the chemical changes the bacteria produce as they multiply. Data are also gathered as to the appearance of the colonies on different media. There are so many kinds of bacteria that even the ones that have been identified for some time have had little attention paid to them. The numbers are just overwhelming and growing every day."

"When I decided to go to med school, I thought I had a good idea of what being a doctor would be like," Frame said with a short laugh. "You know, a nice practice in a modern office. Providing competent diagnosis aided by the abundant medical procedures and medication available. Curing all the medical ills of my patients. Then something like this comes along, and you realize how little you know about so many things. It can be a very humbling experience."

Sitting back on her chair she said, "I hear you went to medical school in Mexico,"

"Yes, I did."

"Why Mexico?"

"I applied to all of the medical schools here but with forty to fifty thousand students trying for fifteen thousand openings your chances are pretty slim even with good grades. Not wanting to wait to reapply, when I was accepted at the Autonomous University, I went."

"That's in Guadalajara, isn't it?"

"Yes," Frame nodded.

"I understand it's quite beautiful there."

"Yes, I was pleasantly surprised. I had spoken to some of the doctors in the Galveston area that had gone there, but I wasn't sure what I would find. I was pleasantly surprised. The houses are all made of stucco and are painted in a rainbow of colors. The bright pinks, greens, and yellows make them look like a huge flower garden set down in the middle of the lakes and mountains that surround Mexico City.

"I'd take trips into the city when I could and walk around the Alameda, the large plaza. I didn't expect to see the modern sky-scrapers and the abundance of hotels."

"Sounds like you got more then a medical education there, Andy."

"I did. Oh man!" said Andy, suddenly glancing at his watch, "I'd better get back to the ER. Thanks for the crash course, Laura."

"Thank you, Andy, for the update, and the tour of Mexico. It's brightened up my day and given me an idea for the perfect vacation spot for my husband and me when this is all over. If you still have some literature from there, I'd like to see it."

"I've got a drawerful. I'll dig it out and drop it off."

Mexico. Why not? Laura thought.

Chapter 16

Day 3

Piedmont Medical Center

Emergency Room Waiting Area

It had been fifty-eight hours since the first patient had arrived at the hospital. At last count there was a total of thirty patients admitted with this still unidentified disease. The lobby and waiting area were now overflowing with family, friends, members of the media, and the curious, all waiting for some word, any word as to the fate of those struck down during the past two days.

There had been more than a few loud shouting matches between hospital staff and terrified family members trying to get some information on the condition of their loved ones. Security had reported two arrests, one a man attempting to sneak into the quarantined ambulance receiving area, resulting in the assault on a security officer. The other one was a member of the press dressed in hospital whites, attempting to gain entrance to the hospital restricted area.

John Singleton was drawn into a confrontation with the family of one of the patients who accused him and the staff of being cold and unfeeling. Nothing was being done they said, and their love ones were left to suffer. Singleton's first reaction was to lash out. But taking a moment to straighten his tie and compose himself, he was able to answer the outcry with as much sympathy as he could. He managed to sit the family down and quietly explain that their welfare, and that of all those involved, was the singular concern of the entire medical staff. Then he went on to promise that he would see to it that they were informed of any change in the condition of their sick.

Television and press stories for the most part had tried to cooperate with hospital efforts, to play down the event to prevent undue panic. But as the hours passed, it was becoming more difficult to assure the public that the situation was not out of control.

Singleton had issued three press releases, and on each occasion had appeared confident that a solution would be found shortly. He had asked everyone to remain calm. Now with the probability of a major storm hitting the area he stood looking out over the rapidly growing crowd. He knew that if they did not resolve this soon the situation could escalate from bad to very bad quickly.

Besides the large number of patients being cared for as a result of this crisis, an increase in auto accidents and cardiac-related cases had caused the emergency room traffic to more than double. Most of these new cases were directly related to the weather. An ever-growing number of personnel and resources were being called upon to meet the challenge.

He knew that if they could not get control soon, additional outside personnel and facilities would have to be brought on line. As always his reputation and the hospital's image were in the back of his mind. He returned to his office and began to put in motion a process that he hoped would provide these services.

Chapter 17

Day 3

County Emergency Communication Center

Lee Reynolds sat at his desk in County Emergency Center. In his capacity as emergency disaster coordinator, he was responsible for coordinating the activities of all the emergency agencies in the county. He also oversaw the joint operations with adjoining counties. Last night he had been alerted and advised that the hurricane center had confirmed hurricane Flora would impact central Virginia. All computer and radar plots predicted that heavy rain, and winds gusting to 110 miles per hour would batter the state within the next thirty-six hours. Even now the leading edge of the storm was producing wind gusts approaching tropical force.

Following emergency protocols, Reynolds had ordered the installation of additional telephones to be available during the storm. A prearranged plan that activated amateur radio operators was initiated to provide critical communications links in the event normal radio and telephone systems failed.

In an hour Reynolds would meet with representatives of fire, rescue, police, Red Cross and social services to set in motion a plan for evacuation, sheltering, and assisting residents affected by this storm. Now he sat and intently studied radar data as they flashed across the computer screen from the direct up-link of the hurricane center.

Looking at a large map on the wall showing all the designated shelter locations, he thought that if this storm stayed on course they could run out of shelter space.

For the past twelve hours a steady rain had been falling. The

James and Rivanna Rivers were beginning to rise. With a storm of this magnitude approaching, it wouldn't be long before these rivers overflowed their banks. Some of the warnings that went out would be unheeded. Some people always thought they could outrun a storm and ended up trapped on roads and bridges.

Reynolds glanced away from the computer screen as the alarm on the teletype machine went off with a loud beep-beep, alerting him to an incoming priority message. Tearing the paper from the machine, he read the boldly printed message.

ATTENTION! All state and local emergency agencies. As of 10:00A.M. this date the Governor has activated the National Guard Units through out the state. Deployment of these units is currently in progress.

He was glad to see it, but he hoped to God they wouldn't need them. His secretary entered the room and announced the arrival of the agency heads.

"Thank you, Adele," he said, acknowledging her. "I'll be there in a minute."

Two hours later he returned to his office. Sitting at his desk, he reviewed the areas that had been covered. The Red Cross and Salvation Army had committed to open and staff five shelters in the district. Arrangements had been made with local supermarkets and drug stores to supply food and fill emergency prescriptions. Fire and rescue units were placed on alert, and all their vehicles were filled with fuel and extra medical supplies. All portable radios had been charged, and spare batteries were provided. A list of all cellular phones with their numbers was compiled and distributed to all agencies.

Selected advance life support personnel were to be provided with emergency response jump bags to place them and their equipment on scenes that might be initially cut off from responding units. Rapid response communications vans were readied to go to isolated areas and act as mobile communications centers.

All hospitals and clinics were surveyed for available personnel, beds, and equipment if needed. Emergency routes into and out of the county and surrounding areas were laid out to ensure the fastest and safest routes out of all affected areas. Satisfied that everything that could be done had been addressed, Reynolds completed his report for county officials. Then he sat back to await the outcome.

Chapter 18

Day 3

Piedmont Medical Center

Infectious Disease Lab

Laura Stewart chronologically listed the events of the past three days. Reviewing the patient charts and lab results, she looked for any common denominator that might explain the wide variation in the patients that were being affected. The ringing of the phone broke her concentration. No doubt it was news of yet another victim, who would only add to the puzzle.

She reached for the receiver as she continued to read the chart before her. "Doctor Stewart here," she said, cradling the phone to her ear.

"Laura, it's Wayne. I think you'd better come down to the unit right away."

"What's the matter, Wayne?" she asked her eyes still scanning a chart. "Have they brought in more patients?"

"No, Laura. It's Bill."

Laura put the clipboard down on the desk before her. "Bill! My husband Bill?"

"Yes, Laura, they just brought him in. He's been in an auto accident on the mountain. The park police that found him said it's been raining hard, and there were strong wind gusts across the mountains. We're evaluating him now."

"Oh, my God! I'll be right down." Hastily replacing the receiver, she took the stairs, not wanting to wait for the elevator.

Collins met her as she entered the unit. "Over here, Laura," he said. "He's in room seven." Hurriedly she followed him into the examining room and stood by the side of the bed.

Turning to Collins, Laura asked, "How bad is it, Wayne?"

"He has a deep laceration over the left eye and there's a good chance of concussion. His left wrist is fractured and he has two cracked ribs. Our immediate concern is a possible ruptured spleen. They're getting ready to move him to the OR."

Taking her husband's hand, she softly called his name. "Bill, can you hear me? It's Laura." His eyelids moved slightly, and she felt him try to squeeze her hand.

"Darling, listen to me," she said leaning close to him. "I'll be right here when you get back from the OR. I've been planning a great vacation for us and don't you dare let me down," she whispered as tears filled her eyes. She gently kissed him on the head and squeezed his hand as she walked along beside the bed. Then she watched as they wheeled him into the elevator and up to the operating room.

Collins placed his hand on her shoulder. "He's in good hands, Laura. I'll have them call you as soon as he's down."

"Thanks, Wayne," she sighed as she walked slowly toward the lounge. Entering, she sat down on a large beige chair, closed her eyes, and placed her head in her hands. As tears slowly ran down her face she prayed softly.

Laura sat motionless, while her mind reeled from the events of the past few days. The frustration they all were feeling had affected everyone in one way or another. She knew in her mind that everyone had done everything in their power to find an answer to this enigma, but she still feared that she had missed something very important.

Now overshadowing all of this was the thought that she and Bill might have waited too long to do the things they had dreamed about since they were married. She remembered all the times they had planned to do something special only to have something in his or her schedules postpone it. The only thing they had not planned for was the unexpected. She thought again of young Kelly Ryman and her husband, planning hopefully for their family, and going out to a town fair for what they thought would be an evening's entertainment.

When this is over, Laura thought to herself, nothing would stop them from spending some quality time together. She glanced at her watch and realized she was not accomplishing anything there. She might as well get back to work.

As she left the lounge, Collins and Frame met her.

"How are you doing?' they asked in unison.

"Thanks, both of you. I'm fine. I was just going back to the lab. I can't just sit here and wait, I'll go crazy."

Look, Laura, why don't you take a break and clear your head?" Collins said. "We wish there was more we could do to help you."

"Thanks, but I'm better off working. I'm going back to take another look at the report from the CDC. I'll bring it down and we can go over it together."

"Good idea," Collins said. "I'll see if Charlie Bennett is free and have him join us in the cafeteria, and we can all have lunch." With the wave of her hand, Laura walked to the elevator.

Waiting to get through to Bennett in neurology, Collins shook his head and said, "Andy, life's painfully unpredictable." Then, in a conscious effort to lighten the tone he continued, "So what's new in your life outside these four walls? Are you still going with that girl you brought to the Christmas party?"

"Yeah, Beth and I got engaged at New Year's, but it'll be a while before we can get married."

"I guess congratulations are in order," Collins said, extending his hand. Andy took the proffered hand and shook it, the smile on his face telling how happy he was.

"Why're you waiting?"

"Well, for one thing, I was waiting to see where my career is going. Truthfully, I was hoping you would consider me for a fellowship position next year in emergency medicine," Andy said, watching Collins closely.

"Well, you're certainly direct," Collins smiled, turning back to confirm the cafeteria meeting with Bennett. Hanging up the phone he put his arm about Andy's shoulder.

Smiling still, he said, "Let's see how you feel after we resolve this situation, and if you haven't changed your mind about emergency medicine, we'll talk about it. Frankly, I'd welcome you to my team. Is Beth on staff here?"

"No, she's in interior decorating and doing very well. Even though we haven't been engaged that long, we've known each other for years. She's been trying for a long time to make an honest man of me. Neither of us is getting any younger, and who knows what the future holds?" Frame laughed as he and Collins went to meet Bennett at the entrance to the cafeteria.

Laura returned to the lab with her mind still on Bill and the operation. Picking up the report, she headed for the cafeteria. After ordering a cup of tea, she joined the men who were seated at a rear table and began to review the report. Looking up, she said, "These results are incredible."

"In what way?" Collins asked.

"Atlanta says that the sample of C. jejuni bacteria we sent them has evolved into a totally new strain. It appears that through some type of accidental gene transfer the bacterium has become extremely virulent."

"Well, they'll get no argument from me on that score," Collins interjected.

"That's not the worst. They go on to say that during the regeneration stage, the bacterium forms spores that protect it from almost all environmental conditions. My God," she muttered in a low voice, almost as if she were thinking out loud, "that means it could be impervious to almost anything we throw at it."

"Do they have any suggestions on how to deal with it?" Bennett asked dryly.

"Nothing specific yet," Laura slowly replied, only half-listening to his question.

"Uh, Laura, are you all right?" Collins asked.

"I'm sorry. It's just that I feel there's something here that we're not seeing, and I can't put my finger on it. Since Bill's accident, I'm having trouble concentrating."

A loud clap of thunder made them jump. Bennett turned to Laura and said, "We all understand what you're going through. With the conditions here for the past few days, it's amazing that any of us is able to concentrate."

Hesitating to see if the celestial fireworks were going to continue, he looked up from his half-eaten sandwich and asked, "What do they say about the characteristics of the bacteria? Do they know how it works?"

"They say it appears to have a built-in defense mechanism," Laura answered as she returned to reading the report. "As it evolves it's encased in what appears to be a pliable spore-like capsule that protects it from any outside contaminants or agents.

"The normal C. jejuni bacterium is very fragile and easily killed, but this strain can withstand heat and changing levels of oxygen and carbon dioxide. Even more frustrating to the lab was its apparent immunity to all classes of antibiotics that it has been subjected to so far."

"So what do we have, some off-beat type of filovirus like ebola or its sister marburg?" Frame asked nervously.

"No, Andy. Though dangerous, I don't believe it's in that class," Laura answered, sensing his anxiety. "Anything that can kill with the speed this can has to be considered a serious threat. I'll need a little more time to digest this report and check out a few ideas I have, then I'll get back with you."

Collins said, "Andy and I will be in the ER if you need us, Laura. I want to call Kate and check on her and the kids. Katlin is terrified of thunderstorms, and we don't know why. When we ask her, she says she just doesn't like the noise. All I know is that every time it storms we have our hands full."

"Thanks, Wayne," Laura said. "Please have them let me know the minute Bill is in recovery."

"You bet," he replied as they walked toward the elevator.

"If you come up with anything new, let me know," Bennett said. "I'll be in neurology."

Back in the ER, Collins sat at the nurse's desk and called Kate. The phone was answered, "Collins residence, may I help you?"

"It's Daddy, Katlin."

"Are you coming home, Daddy? I'm not really afraid, but I'd still like you to come home."

"I can't come right now, honey, but I'll be there as soon as I can."

"When, Daddy?"

"Soon, honey. I love you. Now let me talk to Mommy."

When Kate picked up the receiver, she was out of breath. "Hi, Wayne. How's it going?"

"We're still waiting for answers, and while I had a minute I wanted to see how all of you were doing."

"Katlin is a little nervous, and I was running around closing windows, but we'll be fine. The boys and I are doing everything we can think of to distract her, but you know how she gets."

"I know, honey. I wish I could be there. With this storm moving in, I don't know when I'll get out of here."

"We'll be fine, Wayne. You try and get some rest if you can, and call me when things quiet down. Oh! I had a long talk with Amanda Bennett and by the time we hung up I think she was feeling much better. I told her if she wanted to talk again to just give me a call."

"Thanks, Kate. Take care. I'll call you later."

Chapter 19

Day 3

Piedmont Medical Center

Infectious Disease Control Lab

Laura sat at her desk reading the Atlanta report. She scanned for any detail she might have overlooked. She knew that it was easy to become complacent, believing in the infallibility of personal interpretations, thereby putting limits on what nature could create.

She thought of the countless numbers of bacteria that exist in the heat of deserts, in the extreme cold of the polar ice caps, even in the upper reaches of the atmosphere, flourishing at temperatures high or low enough to kill other forms of life.

Redirecting her attention back to the report, she stood up and walked to the powerful electron microscope in which she had earlier placed a specimen containing the sample sent from Atlanta. She was going to start from the beginning. The answer had to be here.

Atlanta had run a normal MIC (Minimum Inhibitory Concentration) test which exposed the bacteria culture to several antibiotics then selected the ones the sample was sensitive to by determining the amount required to stop the growth of the bacteria undergoing the test.

The most notable difference in the report was that this strain of C. jejuni bacterium, unlike most, was acidic in nature. More puzzling yet was that although it showed sensitivity to several antibiotics in the lab, nothing they had used to date in humans had been effective.

As she studied the picture projected by the electron microscope, she looked closely at the dead specimen of normal C. jejuni bacterium. It appeared as a slender, curved, and motile rod-type bacterium. She then compared it to the culture containing the new mutated species.

This was remarkable, she thought. The structure was completely different. It had evolved into a totally new strain, growing in size by at least 30 sharp, clear, black and white image produced by the electron microscope made it easily distinguishable from the normal strain of bacteria. As she carefully studied the sample, she was drawn to the spore-like shell that encased the bacteria.

Developed in the 1930s, the electron microscope was so named because it directed a beam of electrons rather than light through a specimen. A hot tungsten filament in an electron gun created the beam of electrons. The beams then traveled through the length of the microscope cylinder, housing the lenses, the specimen chamber, and the image-recording system.

The image produced was then projected onto a fluorescent screen or recorded on film. The electron microscope, with its tremendous resolving power, could magnify specimens over 50,000 times.

What did they say about this being different in its chemical makeup? Laura wondered. Then a smile crossed her face as she looked back at the report and read. A major change noted in the evolution of this bacterium was that the coating that now encapsulated it, and the structure of the bacteria itself, appeared to be gram negative, a condition not found in most strains.

"My God! That's it, this could be the answer," she said so loudly she surprised herself. Could it be that simple? she thought as she began to set up an experiment that she hoped would prove her theory.

Carefully she prepared a sample of the culture containing the mutated bacterium and applied an alkaline solution containing a stain that would allow her to see the area in which the solution was drawn. She then moved to a large optical microscope and carefully placed a sample under the lens, staring at it intently.

As she continued to watch, it was apparent that the bacteria's capsule coating was being affected by the solution. She turned on the tape recorder and began to record the information concerning the time and level of change occurring in the new C. jejuni bacterium and its shell.

Then she sat back in amazement. The applied alkaline solution was reacting with the shell, by encasing it. If this process continued it could prevent the release of the bacterium into the system.

That was the answer she had been looking for. Now she knew why Mrs. Warren wasn't affected. It was so basic, they had gone right by it. The infections began once the bacterium was released into the body, although it appeared that might take some time. Returning to her desk, she hastily placed a call to Atlanta.

"Biomedical lab, Doctor Kim."

"Randy, this is Laura Stewart."

"Yes, Laura, how is it going up there? Anything new?"

"I think so, Randy. I'd like you to check something for me."

"What do you need?"

"The mother of one of the first victims of this outbreak was totally unaffected by it. I've been trying to determine why, and I think I may have the answer."

"Go ahead, I'm listening, Laura."

"Randy, when I examined her I found she was being treated for a gastrointestinal condition and was taking several anti-ulcer and antacid medications. I believe that the high alkaline level in her gastrointestinal tract bonded with, or perhaps even calcified the bacterium before its protective shell dissolved, releasing the bacterium into her system."

"If that's the case, Laura, then it would pass harmlessly through the bowel."

"Exactly, but I'd like you to recheck my findings. It might also explain why this new strain might be immune to some or all of the newer antibiotics."

"We're already on it, Laura. We felt the same way you do on

the treatment. We're concerned that the resistance may be caused by plasmid DNA that is resistant to several antibiotics. We're running different combinations now, using both the newer and older prescribed drugs. One other thing you should know, we're attempting to confirm the time required for this strain to fully evolve. We believe it may be as long as twenty-one days, depending on the environmental conditions acting on the bacteria."

"Thanks, Randy, that'll help a lot. I'll notify Doctor Singleton and ask him to set up a staff meeting so I can brief everyone. As you can imagine, there's a lot of concern right now about where we go from here."

"Hang in there, Laura, I'll let you know as soon as we come up with something."

"Thanks again, Randy, we'll be ready to go when you call."

We're going to have to rethink our whole plan, and do it fast, she thought, again peering through the lens of the microscope. Returning to her desk she dialed Singleton's extension. Impatiently she waited for the phone to be answered. It only rang three times before she heard Singleton's voice, but it seemed like an eternity.

"Doctor Singleton, this is Laura Stewart. I must speak with you right away. Will you please arrange for a meeting in conference room A, as soon as possible?"

"If necessary. May I ask why?"

"Not over the phone. It will take some explaining, and time may be running out for us as well as our patients."

"I see, I'll make the arrangements. We'll meet in one hour."

"Fine," she said, She was starting to prepare her notes when the phone abruptly rang. "Doctor Stewart," she said.

"Laura, it's Wayne. They just brought Bill down to recovery."

Chapter 20

Day 3

Piedmont Medical Center Recovery Room

The recovery room was located on the third floor of the medical center. The quiet of the unit was broken by an occasional moan of a recovering patient and the hushed footsteps of the nurses as they moved from bed to bed. Laura eased the door open and was greeted by the on-duty nurse. "I'm Doctor Stewart," she whispered. "My husband was just brought down from the operating room."

"Right this way, doctor. He's still not completely awake. He's been medicated for pain."

Tears clouded Laura's eyes as she stood by Bill's bed. His left eye was covered with a sterile dressing, and they were continuing to monitor him for a possible concussion. The next twenty-four hours would be crucial. His left arm was in a cast from elbow to wrist. The area of most concern was the removal of his ruptured spleen. Laura moved the bed covers aside and checked the dressing.

The nurse placed a chair beside the bed, and Laura gratefully sank into it. She brushed Bill's hair back from his forehead and stroked his whiskered jaw. He moved slightly and opened his eyes.

"What happened?" he asked through parched lips.

Laura smiled through her tears. "You've been in an auto accident. You broke a few bones, and they had to remove your spleen. I'm sure you hurt a lot, and that's partially due to two broken ribs. The surgeon said everything went well, and in a few days you should feel much better."

"What's the good news?" Bill asked, closing his eyes and

drifting into sleep.

The floor nurse returned to her side and whispered to Laura that they would soon move him into a private room, and for now it was best to let him rest. Laura bent over the bed and gently kissed him.

"I'll be back," she whispered.

Following the nurse out into the hall, Laura felt the strain of the past few days. She thought about how close she'd come to losing Bill, and how much she loved him. Seeing him wrapped in bandages and looking so vulnerable made her heart ache.

The nurse took her hand and said, "I know we're supposed to be professionals, but it isn't easy when the patient is one of our own, is it?"

Laura turned away and answered, "No, it's not. I should be in conference room A for at least the next hour. Please call me if there's any change in his condition, will you?"

Chapter 21

Day 3

Piedmont Medical Center Conference Room A

Laura left the recovery room and took the elevator to the main floor. She stopped briefly, glanced into the emergency room, and then continued on to conference room A. Entering she saw Doctor Singleton seated alone at a table in the front of the room. As she approached, Singleton rose and said, "I hope you have some good news for us, doctor. The press is pushing for answers, and so is the community."

Sitting beside him Laura said, "Well, we know a lot more now then we did yesterday. It appears that this strain may have been produced by a totally new formation of genes that we've never seen before."

While they talked, the department chiefs and staff members began to fill the room. All were hopeful of getting some information that would allow them to control this epidemic. There was speculation, too, about the hurricane. Rumors were exchanged about bridges that were nearly under water, of cars spotted by the sides of the roads they had slipped off, of power losses in outlying parts of the county. Noting that the room was full, Doctor Singleton rose from his seat, walked to the front of the room, and stood in front of the microphone.

"Can you hear me in the back? Fine," he said, acknowledging the raised hands in the back of the room. "If you'll be seated we can get started. I have called this meeting at the request of Doctor Stewart from IDC. As most of you know, she has been working closely with the Centers for Disease Control and members of our staff in trying to identify and contain this epidemic.

She will now update all of us on the current situation. Doctor Stewart."

"Thank you, Doctor Singleton," Laura said, stepping to the microphone.

"A lot has transpired since the start of this event three days ago. In the past twenty-four hours we have collectively been able to determine the cause of this infection and how it was introduced into the community. These are the facts as we know them. With the help of the CDC, Health Department and Extension people, we have identified the source as a new and dangerous new strain of the Campylobacter jejuni bacteria. This new mutated bacterial strain is responsible for the infection and related conditions associated with this outbreak.

"It appears that through a chance gene transfer between the bacteria culture applied to the grain being tested by the bioengineers and the normal strain of C. jejuni bacteria found in poultry, a major change in the DNA structure of the bacterium occurred. This resulted in the development of a totally new form of this bacterium. Inasmuch as the culture bacteria used to spray the grain should not have contained any live bacteria, how this process occurred has Atlanta frankly mystified.

"Not only is this strain highly aggressive, but it possesses some unusual properties. For example, in its development stage, the bacterium is protected by a spore-like capsule. This shields it from any environmental condition that would normally affect it, such as heat or cold. Both the bacterium and its shell are considerably more acid-based than would normally be expected. It appears that this protective capsule allows the bacterium to enter the body without being destroyed.

"Once in the body, the bacterium is dormant until it fully evolves, then the outer shell dissolves, releasing it into the gastrointestinal tract. This causes the rapid onset of infection and abdominal distress, resulting in the core temperature rising, causing the high fevers and related cardiac and respiratory conditions we have witnessed. It is, in effect, like a ticking bomb waiting to explode."

Pausing, she said, "Are there any questions on what I've covered before I continue?"

"Yes, I have one," said Doctor Vince Hogan, head of pathology, raising his hand.

"Go ahead, Doctor Hogan," she invited.

"Have you been able to determine the time required for this bacterium to divide and become active? I believe that will help us understand the seemingly random fashion in which this strain has infected the patients."

"You're right, and the answer is no. As you know, most bacteria reproduce by dividing in the middle to form two cells, and they in turn continue to divide. In this case, the division may be occurring as often as every ten minutes or as long as a day. At that rate, millions of bacteria may form from a single bacterium in a period of twenty-four hours or less. Another area of concern is that even in the normal C. jejuni bacteria, the infectious dose is small. As little as four or five hundred bacteria may bring on illness or infection. In this strain even minimal exposure to the bacteria may cause serious illness.

"Atlanta has been working on the problem, and, based on what we have observed so far, we feel that it may be as long as fourteen to twenty-one days before they are released into the system. If that is confirmed, then it could explain the three new cases brought in today and open up the possibility of more to come.

"On the plus side, it appears that the only ones affected by this condition are those that have eaten, or who might eat, the poultry or eggs from that farm. We are working with the Health Department and the Agrotex people to account for and confiscate any additional grain or poultry products involved.

"To follow up on Doctor Hogan's question, the two major areas that Atlanta is pursuing now are, how to immobilize the bacterium before it is released into the body, and how to treat it after it becomes active. The present thinking is that large controlled doses of antacids will bond with or calcify the encapsulated bacterium, inhibiting its release from its shell. This will allow it to pass harmlessly through the bowel. We believe that is what saved Mr. Warren's mother. The second area, and the one of most concern, is the development of an effective treatment to destroy the bacteria once it is active. It appears that it will take a combination of antibiotics given in the proper time and dosage to accomplish this."

"If I may, doctor," interjected Singleton. "I thought we had been doing that with little success.

"That's true," she replied visibly annoyed at the inference. "Atlanta feels, and I agree, that this new strain may be immune to many if not all the new classes of antibiotic drugs. That's why they are running tests with some of the older drugs that have been used in the past to treat similar types of infections."

"Does the center have any idea how long this process may take?"

"No, but they're performing hundreds of computer runs with drugs going back to 1956. They'll contact us as soon as they get a confirmed match."

"If there are no more questions," said Laura, "I'll turn this briefing back to Doctor Singleton. I would like to ask the Health Department team to stay a minute after we adjourn to go over the coordination of a grain confiscation program. Thank you for your attention."

Singleton returned to the microphone. "Thank you, Doctor Stewart. I know how hard you and all the departments have worked during this trying time. I would just like to emphasize that although we are getting closer to containing this event, there are still questions to answer and lives that hang in the balance. On another note, I'm sure that all of you by now are aware of the hurricane approaching us. If the current prediction holds, we may be faced with another event almost as unpredictable as the one we are currently faced with. There is no need, I'm sure, to tell you that such an event will place an even greater demand on this facility and personnel as well as others in the area. I would suggest you contact your families and see to their safety and needs so that we can all concentrate on the task before us. Thank you all. We'll update you as soon as we hear more."

As they walked out of the conference room, Bennett turned to Collins and said, "While we're waiting for the CDC, I'm going up to my office and try to catch up on some of the paper work. Call me if you hear anything."

Chapter 22

Day 3

Office Of Doctor Bennett

Charlie Bennett looked at the pile of paperwork on his desk as he closed the door to his office. It wouldn't get done by looking at it, he thought. Sitting down at the desk, he picked up the top folder and began to read. For the next hour-and-a-half he continued to read files on the affected patients and to make notes. He was halfway through the pile when his secretary buzzed him. He stretched and picked up the phone.

"Yes, Barbara."

"It's your wife, sir. Line one."

"Thank you," he said and pushed the button on the phone. "Amanda, is everything okay?"

"I think I might be in labor, Charlie."

"It's early yet, isn't it?"

"Yes, Charlie. But I started having some pains on and off this morning. Then they got stronger, so I called Doctor Kelsey, and she said to come into the hospital. I called Mrs. Johansen, and she'll keep the boys until you can get them. It's raining harder, and the wind is picking up, blowing debris all over the place. The pains are still coming, so I hope this traffic starts moving."

"Traffic! Amanda, exactly where are you?" Charlie asked with growing anxiety.

"I'm on US 29 South at Airport Road. I'm calling from the cell-phone. I started to drive myself into the hospital, but with this bad weather it looks as if there may be an accident in front of me. Traffic is at a standstill."

"You shouldn't be driving yourself, Amanda. What if you go

into hard labor?" Charlie asked, running his hand through his thinning hair. "Please listen to me. Can you pull out of traffic?"

"Yes, Charlie, I think I can pull onto Airport Road, out of the line of traffic."

"Okay, do that, and I'll send a unit for you. Hold on while I call the dispatcher."

He put her on hold and quickly made the arrangements for the ambulance. He came back on the line and said, "The ambulance will be there shortly."

"Okay, Charlie, see you soon," she said a little wearily. "I'll probably be home again by this evening."

"We'll see," he said, closing his eyes worriedly. "I'll stay on the line with you until help comes. A county police unit should be on the scene shortly."

Amanda maneuvered her car along the shoulder of US 29. As she turned right onto Airport Road the gravel hit the undercarriage of the car. Charlie kept talking while Amanda pulled the car as far off the road as possible and parked it. The sky darkened and the wind increased, as Amanda huddled in the car. Branches were being knocked down, and when one bounced off the roof of the car, she screamed.

"What the hell was that all about, Amanda?" Charlie demanded. "Are the pains coming closer?"

"No, Charlie. I guess this storm has me unnerved. That noise was a tree branch hitting the car and scaring me out of a year's growth."

"Damn," he said, standing up. "Take it easy, now, help should be there soon," he said trying to reassure her.

While they talked, she heard a loud knocking at the car window, and again Amanda jumped. She looked up to see a policeman standing by the car in the pouring rain. "Lady, are you the one having the baby?" he asked.

"Yes, officer, I am," she replied, rolling down the window.

"Just hold on, the ambulance is on the way. We'll get you to the hospital, then we'll see about getting the car moved."

Overhearing this, Charlie said, "Let me talk to him,

Amanda." Doubling over in pain from a new wave of contractions, and without a word, she passed the cell-phone through the window to the policeman.

"Officer, my name is Doctor Bennett, at Piedmont Medical Center. The woman in the car is my wife, and she's in labor. I've dispatched an ambulance to pick her up. I would appreciate it if you could stand by there until the unit arrives. I think she could use the moral support. As soon as she's safe, I'll arrange to have her car moved."

"Okay, doctor. I hear the ambulance coming, I'll stay with her till they arrive, but you'll have to get this car moved soon," he said.

"Thank you, officer."

The officer gave the cell-phone back to Amanda, and within seconds the ambulance was on the scene. Amanda was quickly transferred from her car. With lights flashing and sirens wailing, the ambulance made its way through the traffic toward the hospital.

Bennett placed the receiver back on the cradle and watched the rain form spiral patterns on the window. He picked up the next file on his desk and stared blankly at it. That was the end of this for now, he thought, placing the folder back on the pile and walking out of the office. On the way past his secretary's desk, he stopped and told her where he'd be if anyone needed him. Then he headed for the elevator and maternity on the eighth floor. The elevator came to a halt, and as the door slid open Charlie came face to face with Linda Kelsey, a pleasant woman in her middle forties with short brown hair and thick glasses.

"Doctor Kelsey, just the person I'm looking for," he said.

"Relax, Charlie," she said. "I know Amanda is on the way in, I talked to her a little while ago. I also know she's two weeks early, but when she arrives I'll examine her and see where we go."

They had barely finished talking when the elevator doors opened again and Amanda was wheeled off. Charlie bent down and took her hand in his. "How are you?" he asked, as Doctor

Kelsey took her other hand and said, "Let me have a few minutes to check her over and I'll call you in."

With a quick kiss Charlie let go of Amanda's hand and Doctor Kelsey walked beside her into the labor and delivery unit.

Amanda was helped onto the examining table where her clothes were removed and replaced with a hospital gown. The nurse placed her legs into the stirrups and the doctor began her examination. Kelsey knew that Amanda was nervous and tried to reassure her that everything was normal. The amniotic sack broke just as Kelsey was finishing the exam but she knew it could still be hours before the baby was born.

Amanda's bedding was changed and Charlie was called in. He went to the bed and put his arms around his wife and he looked about at all the equipment in the room. When the twins had been born he wasn't allowed in the room and hadn't seen what went on. Today things were different; not only was he in the room but also expected to help his wife through the whole procedure.

"This could take some time yet," said Doctor Kelsey to both of them. "Amanda, I ordered an epidural."

"Okay, doctor," Amanda said holding her breath as the contractions stared again. Kelsey proceeded to prepare her for the anesthesiologist. Doctor Mark Hill inserted a thin catheter into the lower part of Amanda's back and injected a local anesthetic that would cause numbness from the waist down.

"This will wear off by the time the worst is over, and by that time your baby will be born," he told Amanda.

"I hope you're right," she said. "I didn't have this when the twins were born and I felt every piercing pain."

Two hours later Charlie was wiping the perspiration from Amanda's face. The strain had begun to tell. Doctor Kelsey checked her patient again and said, "All right Amanda, I want you to relax."

Another hour went by and Charlie was sweating as much as Amanda. "I can't do this any more," Amanda said.

"You're doing great, Mandy," said Charlie. Suddenly she squeezed his hand so tightly he winced "What's happening?" he asked, looking at Doctor Kelsey.

"She's beginning to crown. All right now, Amanda, push," said Kelsey. Bearing down with all of her strength Amanda pushed and felt relief as the baby's head popped into Doctor Kelsey's hands. The involuntary uterine contractions from Amanda had pushed the baby completely out. Kelsey quickly suctioned the mouth and nose and held the child upside down until she began to cry. Then she clamped and cut the umbilical cord.

The attending nurse took the baby, weighed and measured her, and gave her back to Doctor Kelsey.

"There," she said holding the baby up for all to see. "You have a beautiful baby girl. Do you have a name for her?"

Charlie and Amanda looked at the red squealing child and answered in unison, "Deborah!" Then Charlie said, "She'll be as beautiful as her mother," and hugged Amanda.

The nurse quickly wrapped the baby in a small blanket and gave her to Charlie, while Kelsey attended to Amanda.

Taking the baby from Bennett, Kelsey said, "Why don't you go buy some cigars or something, Charlie, while we get your wife and daughter cleaned up."

Before he could answer, there was a bright flash of lightning, followed by a loud clap of thunder. "I get the message, he said. I'll see you later."

Chapter 23

Day 3

Piedmont Medical Center

Bill Stewart's Room

Laura Stewart had been sitting for ten minutes by the side of her husband's bed when he awoke. "You look much better now than when they brought you in here," she said, taking his hand in hers.

Bill smiled ruefully, but was not too cheerful; he was still in a lot of pain. "You know, all I kept thinking about in those few seconds the car was rolling down that hill was that I might not see you again, and that we had spent more time lately arguing with each other than doing the things that really matter."

"I know," Laura agreed. "When Wayne called me and told me that you'd been brought in, the last five years of our life flashed before me. That's all going to change, I promise you Bill. When you get back on your feet, we're going to take a long vacation, and I think I've found the perfect place."

Bill looked distantly at Laura. "Are you in pain?" she asked.

"Some," he answered. "I just have trouble believing things will be any different, that we'll ever have more time together."

"I'm really going to try this time, Bill," Laura answered softly. The sound of Laura's pager interrupted their conversation.

"It's the IDC lab," she said looking at the number. "I hope this is the call I've been waiting for." Picking up the phone on the bedside table, she hastily dialed the number.

After two rings, she heard, "IDC lab, Conway."

"This is Doctor Stewart, I was paged."

"Oh yes, Doctor Stewart, Doctor Kim from the CDC called, He wants you to call him back as soon as possible."

"Thanks, Conway. I'll be there shortly."

She hung up the receiver and turned back to Bill. "This could be the information we've needed from Atlanta to control this thing. I have to go," but then seeing Bill turn his head away, she realized what he must have been thinking. Quickly she added, "But I can stay a few minutes, long enough to tell you about the vacation I've planned."

Still grimacing from the pain Bill looked back at her, and asked, "Where did you have in mind?"

"I was talking to one of the interns today, and he spent four years in Mexico at a medical school. Bill, the description he gave of the area was breathtaking. White sand, blue water, and margaritas. It sounds like just the kind of place where we can relax and just get to know each other again.

"Andy, the intern I was talking about, said he would drop off some brochures."

"If it makes you that excited just talking about it," Bill said, squeezing her hand, "I can't wait to go. I'll get the tickets as soon as I'm back on my feet."

"Great." Just then all the lights flickered in the room and in the corridor. She heard a muffled exclamation and the words "power" and "hurricane."

She walked over to the window. The wind-driven rain pelted the window and ran in streams across the sill. The hospital's emergency power had been activated, but as far as she could see, except for the hospital, everything was in darkness. From where she stood she couldn't tell if the blackout was due to the lightning strike or an accident.

"I'm sorry, Bill, but I've got to call down to the ER."

She picked up a house phone and dialed. When her call was answered, she asked for Collins. Hearing his voice, she said, "Wayne, this is Laura. What's going on down there?"

"We're on emergency power," he replied. "The air-conditioning and fans are out, and we have a packed house with a lot of nervous patients."

"I'm coming down," she said.

Hanging up, she turned back to Bill. "I'm sorry, darling, but I've got to get down to the ER. I'll be back as soon as I can." She leaned over to kiss him. "I promise." He turned his cheek to her lips and she heard him mumble something.

"What?" She asked.

"I said, I can taste those margaritas now."

With the added impact of the storm and the power outage, the hospital, already running with increased staff to deal with the epidemic, was doubling its efforts. Additional personnel from all areas were called in to deal with the increasing demand for medical assistance. The failure of a major power grid had plunged the entire area into darkness.

Primary care areas of the hospital, including the operating room, intensive care unit and critical care unit had their own battery-powered backup and were functioning normally. All other areas were operating on emergency power. Much of the ER and floor equipment was running on internal battery power. All nonessential equipment including passenger elevators was out of service. Downstairs, as she passed the entrance door, Laura saw large puddles of water forming outside. Tree branches were down, and the increasing wind gusts were buffeting the entrance with a driving rain. She saw the flashing red lights of yet another ambulance as it left the hospital. Where were they going and would they find?

In the ER she was astounded to see the number of patients waiting for attention. All the available beds were full, and patient-filled Gurneys were lined against the walls.

Chapter 24

Day 3

County Emergency Communication Center

The Emergency Communication Center had been fully staffed and operational for the past several hours. Lee Reynolds had frequent meetings with representatives from Emergency Services, Red Cross, and other service agencies, ensuring that no area was left unguarded. All possible situations were being addressed. The five radio dispatch desks that handled all the police and rescue calls for the county were beehives of activity. There had been fifteen auto accidents reported, eight of them requiring medical assistance. In addition, there had been cardiac calls, and numerous reports of flooding in low-lying areas. The Fire Department was being kept busy too.

An additional bank of twenty telephones rang continuously as reports of power outages, downed trees, gas leaks, flooding, and other problems not requiring 911 intervention came in.

Red Cross and Salvation Army shelters had been activated in Albemarle, Fluvanna, Louisa, and surrounding counties. More emergencies were expected in other counties as the eye of the storm moved closer.

Due to the rapidly rising levels of the James and Rivanna Rivers and the many streams that traversed the area, heavy flooding had caused the closure of sections of several major highways. Many secondary and private roads were also impassable due to the torrential rains that had been sweeping the area. Emergency communication vans had been set up in strategic locations to act as mobile command centers, providing rapid communications to hospitals and to communication centers located throughout the counties.

Back at his desk, Lee Reynolds' attention was drawn to the teletype machine grinding out a priority message. What now, Lee thought, as he watched the message being typed out. He glanced down at the paper and read.

As of 2:00 P.M. the hurricane forecast center places the eye of hurricane Flora fifty miles north of Charlotte, N.C. moving at 15 MPH in a north by northeast direction. Hurricane force winds with gusts of 100 MPH extend 50 miles from the eye. Tropical force winds extend 200 miles. Hurricane warnings are posted as far north as Baltimore.

It's beginning to weaken, Reynolds mused. That's something to be thankful for. He reviewed the damage reports beginning to litter his desk. There was going to be a big mess to clean up in the morning, he thought, and the power outages would slow everything down.

He heard that the Medical Center was already overburdened and working on emergency power. Thank God for that, he thought, turning his attention to the night ahead.

"How are we looking?" Reynolds asked Sue Carter, the 911 supervisor.

"So far, so good," Carter replied. "I'm bringing in extra people to relieve on the positions and answer the telephones. As the storm gets closer the volume of calls is increasing tremendously. We're maintaining communications with all emergency centers in the surrounding counties."

"Good." Reynolds nodded approvingly. "The more lines of communications we have between areas the faster we'll be able to dispatch help. We want to have all our bases covered. Past disasters, like the flood and road collapse in Green and Madison Counties, made us realize how quickly an area can be cut off."

While they talked, the senior dispatcher handed Carter an updated report of the calls received since the start of the shift. Frowning, she looked up at Reynolds.

"Looks like it's already beginning," she said. "We've had a number of auto accidents that require medical assistance. And there've been five cardiac-related calls, ten reports of flooding in low-lying areas, and the list goes on. The Fire Department has also responded to five house fires directly connected to the storm."

"Sue, I hate to drop anything else on you, but I got a call from the Medical Center administrator. He's very worried about the effects this storm will have on their handling of the current epidemic. He's asked that the communication center notify the hospital whenever an ambulance responds to a call related to the epidemic, so that isolation can be maintained."

"Okay, Lee. I'll do the best I can."

"Thanks, Sue."

"Lee," called Carter as he was leaving. "The latest weather update is coming in."

"Coming," he said. Reaching the teletype machine, he watched with Sue as the message was printed out.

As of 400 PM EST the Hurricane Forecast Center advises that hurricane Flora is now headed in a more northerly direction. Top winds are down to 80 MPH the eye is expected to pass 50 miles west of Charlottesville, sending it over the mountains. This should cause it to lose strength rapidly.

"Yes!" said Reynolds, raising his arm in a victory gesture. "If this forecast is accurate, what we're getting now should be the worst we'll see. The next three hours will tell the tale."

Carter moved cautiously through the maze of tables, wires, and telephone equipment that filled the center. "Amen to that" she said. "I'll have this latest advisory put out over the air to all agencies."

Chapter 25

Day 3

Piedmont Medical Center

Infectious Disease Lab

When Laura Stewart returned to the lab from the ER, she was tired but hopeful. She grabbed a pad and dialed the CDC. She was hoping they had found what made this thing tick as she anxiously waited for the call to go through.

"Biomedical lab, Doctor Kim."

"It's Laura Stewart, I received your message. Sorry I didn't get back to you sooner, but we're on emergency power and running our legs off, trying to keep up with the heavy patient load. I hope you've got some answers for us."

"I think so. Everything we've done here says it should work. Now it's going to be up to you to find out. How long do you think it will take you get a handle on things up there? Are you in the eye yet?"

"No, that's still a few hours off, but we're ready to implement whatever you have for us."

"Okay, here it is. We ran everything we had through the data banks and asked for possible combinations of drugs that might be effective against this strain. Then we ran additional MIC tests to see which ones had the highest probability of success. Our feeling is that a combination of older drugs from the late sixties, in higher doses, should effectively kill the bacteria. I'll give them to you verbally, but we'll be faxing the full report and recommendations to you momentarily."

"Nice job. Give me what you have, and I'll get started right away. As soon as the hard copy gets here, I'll have it distributed to the staff. I'm ready to copy, go ahead."

"Laura, I think we're agreed that you're going to have to treat both aspects of this event to make sure it's effectively neutralized."

"Yes, Randy," Laura said. "We've both agreed that we're actually fighting two events."

"Right. Our tests indicate that appropriate doses of Bactrim according to weight and Doxycycline administered in separate IV solutions for at least forty-eight hours should kill the bacteria and control the infection."

"Doxycycline and Bactrim," Laura exclaimed. "I guess we'll find out if what they say about old way sometimes being the best is true in this case. It's hard to find a needle in a haystack when you're still looking for the haystack. You guys did a great job."

"Thanks. It's imperative that those individuals who have ingested the poultry, eggs or anything made with the eggs purchased from the farm in the past three weeks are also treated with high doses of antacids and anti-ulcer medication. That should neutralize the bacteria not yet released and allow it to pass safely though the intestine, and through the bowel, as in the case of Mrs. Warren. With the prolonged incubation period of this strain, if they aren't treated soon you're likely to lose more people."

Laura reflected a moment on what he had told her and said, "You've confirmed my worst suspicions, Randy. We're going to need help from the media, the Health Department, and the police in getting the message out to everyone in the area that may have been exposed. I'll work up the schedule for administering the medication, and ask Dr. Singleton to coordinate the notification procedure."

"Good luck, Laura," he replied. "Remember, we're just a phone call away if you need us."

"Thanks, Randy, we'll keep you posted." Hanging up, she went mentally through her message to Dr. Singleton. They had to hit all the media, there was no time to lose. Gathering the sheets from the fax machine she began to prepare the treatment that would, God willing, end this epidemic. Her thoughts were interrupted by a lab tech apologizing to someone for coming in late. "Getting ready for work, I learned how dependent I am on electricity," the woman said.

"Is your power out, too?" her supervisor asked.

"Haven't you heard? It's not just the Medical Center and the area around here. The whole county has lost its power."

Chapter 26

Day 3

Piedmont Medical Center Isolation Ward

After writing up instructions for the floor staff, Laura called Collins. "Wayne, I know you have your hands full down there," she said "but I need your help. I just got off the phone with Randy Kim at the CDC."

"I hope he had something good to tell us Collins," said.

"Yes, he did," Laura assured him. "They've worked up a treatment for us to use, and they believe it will do the job."

"That's the best news I've heard all week," he sighed.

"I want to get started right way."

"How can I help, Laura?"

"I know you can't leave the ER now, but if you can spare Andy for a while, it would be a great help. I'm sure the floor staff and the two of us can initiate this treatment. I've already had them go over the charts to check for any allergies to the drugs we'll be using. If we don't find any, we're ready to go."

"Okay, Laura, I'll send Andy right up, and good luck. I'll get up there as soon as I can, and you can fill me in."

"Thanks, Wayne, we'll look for you later."

Ten minutes later, Laura entered the ward and approached the desk. Though she was as tired as the rest of the staff from the long hours they had all been working, her eyes were filled with excitement.

"I hear you have heard from the CDC, Laura," Frame said, entering the ward behind her.

"Doctor Kim has come up with a combination of drugs for us to use in IV solutions. I'd like to get started on it right away."

Grinning widely, unable to contain his relief, Andy pulled on a pair of sterile gloves and said, "Okay! Let's do it!"

"Here's what Atlanta has suggested," she said, passing him the notes she had taken from Kim. Frame quickly read over the notes. Somewhat surprised, he said, "I guess because these are older drugs, we never considered giving them, even in higher doses. I'm sure Atlanta put a lot of time into this, so let's get started."

"Agreed," Laura replied. "Atlanta has worked up what they feel should be the proper dosage of each drug to effectively destroy the bacterium. We believe we should administer five hundred milligrams of Doxycycline in one hundred cc of normal saline IV, along with three ampules of Bactrim in 250 milliliters IV of 5 percent dextrose solution twice a day. Also, high doses of Mylanta and bicarbonate, coupled with thirty milligrams of Omeprazole. This should neutralize nonactive bacteria still present in their systems.

"I've had the charts checked for any allergies to the drug. None have been found, so we'll set up the IVs, two to each patient."

For the next two hours, Laura, Andy, and the three floor nurses, went about methodically setting up the IVs and administering the prescribed drugs. The medication was noted on the charts at the foot of each bed. When they had finished, Laura sighed, and said, "Now we wait, and pray that this combination works."

"How long do you think it will take before we see any results?" Andy asked.

"Well, each patient will react differently, but we should know something within the next twelve hours, I hope. I'll call Doctor Singleton and ask him to take care of coordinating the activities of the Health Department, police, and media in carrying out the second phase of the treatment. With the power out all over the county, this is going to take some doing."

Two nurses checked the patients and adjusted the drip on a few of the IVs. Then Laura and Andy left the ward.

John Singleton had sent his secretary home and was about to leave the office himself when the phone rang. He walked toward the office door while the phone continued to ring. Hesitating, he put down his briefcase and reached for the receiver.

"Singleton," he snapped.

"This is Doctor Stewart, I'm glad I caught you."

"Doctor Stewart, I didn't expect to hear from you any more today. Is there a problem?"

"On the contrary, I hope we may have a solution. I talked to Doctor Kim at the CDC," she said, and continued to relate the procedure that they had discussed.

"Now, sir," she continued, "I need your help in contacting the Health Department and the media to ask that they help us contact all the people who attended the County Fair or who may have purchased chickens or eggs from the Warren farm in the past thirty days."

"Do you think we ought do that now? I mean, shouldn't we wait and see if the combination of drugs works first?" Singleton queried. "And do you realize that the power is out all over this county?"

"I'm well aware of that," Laura acknowledged. "But we have to get the word out. This combination will take at least twelve hours or more before we even begin to see results. It's imperative that we notify anyone else who may have been exposed to this bacterium. If we start them on preventive medication of high antacids, we think it will counteract the bacteria that have not yet activated in their systems. Hopefully, if we catch it soon enough, we can prevent further outbreaks of this illness."

Singleton nervously twisted the phone cord through his fingers as he listened to Stewart. When she had finished, he hesitated for a moment, then said, "I'll see whom I can reach tonight."

"Thank you, sir."

Singleton hit the disconnect button and redialed. It was a long shot, but maybe he could catch Ken Sterling at the Health Department. Ferreting out all the people who might have been infected, in the dark, in a hurricane, without the aid of radio and television would be quite a job. Stewart was right, there was no choice.

Finishing his calls, he glanced at his watch. It was 9:45 P.M. That was all he could do tonight. He turned off the lights and locked the door behind him. Pausing at the bulletin board, he posted a notice calling for an 8:00 A.M. press conference and left the hospital.

Chapter 27

Piedmont Medical Center

Bill Stewart's Room

Laura left the nurse's station and started for the elevator, then stopped abruptly when she remembered the power failure had put them out of service. She opened the exit door and took the stairs to the fifth floor and the E. Wing. Visiting hours were over, and most of the patients were settled in for the night. She walked into Bill's room and saw that he was propped up in bed reading a National Geographic.

The bandages over his left eye had been removed, leaving a visible red scar. The cast on his left wrist would remain for at least four weeks, and the broken ribs would take time healing. He reached for her with his good hand as she sat on the side of his bed and leaned over and kissed him on the lips.

"You look much better tonight," she said, smiling with relief.

"I do feel better. As long as I remember not to move too quickly and jar the ribs, the doc says I'll be fine. The scars from the operation will heal, and before you know it, the accident will only be a memory. Now all we need is to get you out of here," he said, crinkling his scarred brow.

"That's one of reasons I'm here," Laura said. "I've just come from the isolation ward. The CDC called earlier with what we hope is an answer. They gave us a combination of drugs in IV solution. All the affected patients are being medicated and watched. We're very encouraged about this. The next twelve hours will be crucial. I'll stay here for a while, and then check on them again. Have you given any more thought to that vacation in Mexico?"

Bill pulled her closer to him on the bed. "I've been lying here thinking about us, and Mexico sounds great. Maybe by the time I'm ready to leave here we'll have some serious plans made."

"I think it could be a wonderful trip," she said. Then, kissing him, she stood at the head of the bed. "I have a call I have to make, then I'm going to try to get some rest. Why don't you do the same, and I'll see you tomorrow."

Chapter 28

Day 4

Piedmont Medical Center

Isolation Ward

After catching a few hours of restless sleep Laura woke still tired and groggy. Getting up from the cot, she brushed some of the wrinkles from her clothes. She washed her face and neck with cold water, ran a comb through her hair, and clipped it in place at the back of her head. You are a sight, Laura Stewart, she mused as she left the lounge. She stopped by the nurse's station and poured a cup of three-hour-old coffee, drank it black, and headed for the isolation ward.

At the nurse's desk she put a fresh gown on over her clothes and entered the ward. She was pleased by the report of the charge nurse--most of the patients had spent a restful night.

Last night when she had left the ward, all of the patients had been very quiet. Now she was astounded to see movement. Some patients were awake and asking questions, while others lay quietly but watching the activity in the room. She made her way from bed to bed until she came to Kelly Ryman. The young woman was awake and alert. Laura stopped beside her. "Good morning, Kelly, how do you feel?"

"Better, I think."

"That's good to hear, Kelly."

"The past few days everything was far away and I wasn't sure I would ever completely wake up again," Kelly said. "Today things seem clearer, I feel that I'm back among the living."

"Good!" Laura said.

"Doctor Stewart, how's my baby? Can I see her please? Where is Bobby?"

"Slow down! First, I looked in the nursery last night and your little girl appears to have had no serious effects from this illness."

"Thank God," Kelly sighed.

"Second, your husband has been visiting both of you constantly. He went home to get some rest, and he'll be so happy to see you awake. Third, I'll see what arrangements can be made to move you into a private room so you can see Bobby and the baby up close, okay?"

"You've been so kind," said Kelly reaching out to grasp Laura's hand.

"It's my pleasure. You rest now, Kelly. I have to check on the others and then I have a meeting to attend, but I'll be back soon, I promise."

The IVs would run for at least thirty-six hours. To prevent the possibility of any dormant bacteria becoming active, high doses of antacids would also be administered. Some of the worst cases might take seven to ten days of treatment, but now there was light at the end of the tunnel.

With things progressing so well in the isolation ward, Laura's thoughts turned to Bill. She hoped that this trip to Mexico would bring them closer together. It should give them a chance to work out the problems caused in their lives by their conflicting obligations. She hadn't been this excited about a vacation in a long time.

As Laura entered the stairway she saw Bob Ryman. "Is something wrong, Bob? You look upset."

Bob hung his head sheepishly. "No, doctor, I'm fine. It's just that we have a flood in our basement from the storm, and Kelly's doll collection was soaked pretty bad. After all she's been through she doesn't need any more bad news, and I don't know how to tell her. I guess that's minor after the past few day's."

"I don't mean to laugh, Bob, but I don't think Kelly will be too upset over that right now."

126

"I guess it was pretty silly, but I've been so worried about Kelly and the baby that I've lost all sense of balance."

Laura smiled, and reassured him that both Kelly and the baby would be fine, and when this was over they would be able to get on with their lives.

Leaving Bob she continued on her way. She now felt less concerned about her own situation, and more confident that Bill's and her feelings for each other would see them through this unsettling time, for like the epidemic it was coming to an end. Then almost as a sign of confirmation, the lights flicked and power was restored to the hospital.

Chapter 29

Day 4

Piedmont Medical Center

Main Conference Room

At precisely 8:00 a.m. the meeting was called to order. John Singleton, always the administrator, in a three-piece suit and snowy white shirt, patted his silver hair and looked out over the crowded room. He was pleased to see that all of his calls from the night before had been answered. Attending were Ken Sterling and his associates from the Health Department, members of the media, emergency services, and the Red Cross. TV cameras were set up along the sides of the conference room along with newspaper and radio people.

He took a sip of water from the glass on the podium and tapped the microphone for attention. The noise in the room was stilled, and Singleton began.

"Ladies and gentlemen, considering the current weather and the many situations you have had to deal with in the past several days, I hope this will be the last time I need to call you to the Medical Center about this epidemic. With me this morning are Doctors Laura Stewart of Infectious Disease, Wayne Collins, chief of emergency medicine, Charlie Bennett, chief of neurology, as well as the many staff members involved with this since its onset. Let me explain what's happened and why I've asked you here today.

"Last night, Doctor Stewart called me after she received a call from the CDC in Atlanta. They have recommended a combination of drugs that have been administered to all of the patients in our isolation ward. I personally checked on these cases this morning and am happy to report that most of the affected people are showing signs of improvement.

"What we now need from the Health Department and the media is help in reaching anyone who has either been at the County Fair and eaten chicken or eggs, or who has purchased chicken or eggs from the Warren farm in the past thirty days. These people must come in to the center for treatment immediately. If anyone has bought poultry or eggs and has not used them, please don't. We urge them to contact the Health Department, which will advise them on what action to take. We must get started on this right away.

"Of course, as you know, the electric company has not yet been able to restore all the power that has been lost throughout the county. Downed trees, widespread debris, and unpassable roads are hindering their efforts. As a result, contacting those people who might have purchased or used the infected poultry and eggs is an additional challenge. The police and sheriff's departments have agreed to do a door-to-door survey and to provide transport if necessary, and I hope that you will offer them your full cooperation.

"We want to stress that this only involves anyone who was at the fair, or who obtained chickens or eggs at the Warren farm. The illness is not contagious, so there's no need for alarm. This is another area in which you, especially those in the media, can be of assistance to us, making sure that this part of our message gets across as well. Thank you all for your assistance in dealing with this emergency, and those related to the storm."

Singleton finished his glass of water and stepped to the floor to mingle with the assembled group.

Chapter 30

Day 5

Agrotex Research Laboratories

Doctor Tyler Wilson's Office

Doctor Tyler Wilson sat at his desk and slowly turned the pages of the lengthy report he had received on the retesting of the treated grain. The tests run had duplicated the original in every detail. The results showed no significant change in either the bacterium or the poultry involved. The birds included in the tests had been closely monitored. The grain had been screened for even the slightest change from its original state. The chickens had been observed for any change in their egg-laying ability as well as any physical discomfort or illness during the entire test period, and still no significant change in their condition was noted.

To be doubly sure of their findings, chickens were killed and pathology examinations were performed. No traces of the mutated C. jejuni bacteria were discovered. Samples were then sent to the state lab in Richmond to substantiate their findings. Wilson was greatly disturbed by this. He was uncomfortable with the fact that they could not recreate the mutation in the C. jejuni bacteria. He had ordered his people to go back over every step of the test and note even the slightest difference that might have occurred. Still scanning the report, he reached for his ringing phone.

"Doctor Wilson, this is Dan Wagner in the lab. We found something I think you had better see."

"I'm on my way," Wilson replied. Pulling his jacket from the back of the chair and hastily leaving the office, he hope this was what they had been looking for. They could use some good news about now.

Reaching the elevator, he pushed the call button and paced up and down in front of the door impatiently. He pushed the button again. "Damn elevator," he said out loud, opening the exit door and taking the stairs down three floors to the research area.

Entering the lab, he said, "What have you found, Dan?"

"Two things that might be connected to the failure of the first test," replied Wagner. "First, in comparing temperatures we noticed that there was a five degree control temperature difference between the first and second cultures."

"What!" interrupted Wilson. "Why wasn't that noticed during the preparation phase?"

"Well, it appears that we had gotten cross-information," Wagner said, hesitantly. "The thermometers showed the correct temperature, but when we checked the graph recorder we found the mismatch."

"Good Lord!" exclaimed Wilson. "What else did you find?"

"I think the best way to explain it would be to show you. If you look at the slide under the high resolution microscope, you'll notice two samples."

"Yes, I see them," said Wilson. "One is a spore-producing bacillus and one is not. What's the point?"

"The point is that they're from the same culture, the one used during the first test."

"That's impossible," snapped Wilson looking up from the microscope. "The bacillus culture used for that test carried a defective gene that prevented the formation of spores. How do you explain that?"

"Frankly, sir, I don't know what to make of it. If I had to guess, I would say that somehow, during the development of the culture, the addition of one or a possible combination of the additives and the warmer incubation temperature acted in some way on the bacillus that resulted in the repair of the defective gene."

"Oh God, Dan! Are you telling me that the culture we sprayed on the grain may have contained live spores?"

"I'm afraid so, sir. We followed the same procedure we've used in all the other programs right down to the final sterilization of the culture before spraying. There was nothing to indicate that anything was wrong."

Wilson looked up from the microscope and said with resignation, "I'd better go up to Sampson's office and let him know what's happened. Lord knows, I don't want him to get it second hand. You know, Dan, Frank always had reservations about this project, and it was only because I assured him that the risks would be minimal that he allowed the project to continue. I convinced him that it could be very beneficial to the poultry and bovine industry."

"I know, sir," Dan replied. "All of us in the lab were very optimistic. The outlook from previous tests was more than promising."

"Right now, Dan, we'd better concentrate on what effect this error has had on those involved, and what can be done to see that it doesn't happen again.

"I want a full report on these findings on my desk in the morning. I'll contact all the agencies involved tomorrow. Maybe if we get on this right away we can overcome some of the reaction that is sure to come." Looking into the microscope again, he turned and left the lab.

Wilson returned to his office and placed a call to Frank Sampson, the company president. He told him he was on his way up to discuss an urgent matter. He gathered the files from the project from his desk, left the office, and took the elevator to the top floor He stepped from the elevator and walked down the hall. He paused outside the door and read the gold nameplate: "Frank Sampson, President."

Wilson entered and was acknowledged by the secretary. With a nod of greeting she said, "Go right in, Doctor Wilson, he's waiting for you."

As the door closed behind Wilson, Sampson rose from the

big red leather chair behind the glass-top desk, and extended his hand in greeting. "I haven't seen much of you lately, Tyler. Have a seat and tell me what's so urgent."

"I know, Frank," Wilson replied. "After you hear what I have to say, you may not want to see me again." He settled uncomfortably in the chair.

"Well, whatever it is, Tyler, I hope it will answer some of the questions I've been getting. I've already had three calls from the legal department, and several from the media. How bad is it?" Sampson asked.

"Regrettably, Frank," replied Tyler, "we did, though unintentionally, provide the catalyst that may have created an unbelievable epidemic."

Sitting back in his chair, Sampson said quietly, "You'd better lay it all out for me, Tyler."

For the next two hours Tyler Wilson reviewed the entire project with Sampson. Concentrating on the meticulous precautions that had been taken, and trying to account for the missed observations that now appeared to have brought about this incredible development.

With the report finished, Tyler rose and walked to the window. Turning back to Sampson, he said, "Frank, we all know that this could happen to any company, anywhere, but it happened here, on my watch, and on my recommendation. Because of that, your reputation, and the company's, may now be on the line. We probably still don't know the effect this occurrence has had on the families of those who have died, or were made ill. As far as I'm concerned, the buck stops here. I'll stay on, if you wish, to help resolve the technical and legal ramifications that will surely come from this, and then I'll resign. You can bring in a new director."

Sampson rose from his chair and stood next to Wilson, who was staring blankly out the window. Placing his arm on his shoulder, he said, "Let's not make any hasty decisions Tyler, until we know all of the facts."

Chapter 31

Day 5

County Emergency Communication Center

Lee Reynolds leaned back in his chair, stretched his long legs, and rubbed his bloodshot eyes. He, with the rest of his staff and volunteers, had ridden out the worst of the storm in the communications center. He looked around the room, littered with empty coffee containers and sandwich wrappers. He turned to Sue Carter, seated at the next desk, and said, "It's been one hell of an experience."

"That's putting it mildly," Carter said, smiling. "All things considered, I guess we were lucky. It could have been a lot worse."

Though Hurricane Flora had now been downgraded to a tropical storm and had not come as close as expected, nevertheless, the winds accompanied by heavy rain had caused a lot of damage. Power was out over much of the area, and waterlogged loblolly pines had fallen like toothpicks, blocking roads and causing many accidents. The rains had continued until 5:00 a.m. Wind gusts were still blowing debris around the streets. Newscasters were cautioning listeners to be careful driving on water-covered roads and to watch for downed trees and wires. Repair crews were out throughout the area.

Assessment had begun early, and by 7:00 a.m. small aircraft from the Civil Air Patrol, a nearby Coast Guard auxiliary' air unit, as well as aircraft from the state police and other agencies had been requested to provide visual and photographic information on damage caused by the passing storm. This information would be used to prioritize the areas according to the damage and the equipment that would be needed to restore power and clean up debris from downed trees and flood waters.

The Red Cross had sheltered dozens of people throughout the five counties and was now arranging for permanent housing for those who had lost their homes and possessions due to flooding and fires. The shelters would remain open for the next couple of days or until everyone had been accounted for and all services were restored to the community.

The Federal Emergency Management Agency (FEMA) personnel were also in the area to assist in the recovery process.

Telephone and power company crews that had been working through the night were trying to replace all the poles and wires that had been damaged in the storm.

A watery sun peeped from behind gray clouds, and the forecast was sunny and dry for at least the next few days. With the air reconnaissance reports coming in, Lee Reynolds, Sue Carter, and their staff had a good overall view of what needed to be done to aid in the cleanup. While they reviewed the reports, the volunteers began to clean up the coffee and food containers that were strewn on the tables. Others had the task of rolling up and storing the cables used to connect the emergency telephones. It was possible now to cross the room without fear of tripping. The floor was being swept and the teletype messages had been put in a neat pile on Reynolds' desk.

Turning to Carter, he said, "I don't know about you but I could use some fresh air. I'm going outside to see what kind of a mess we have."

Leaving the Command Center, they walked down the long corridor leading to the outside doors. Reynolds opened the door, and they walked out into the street. A sanitation truck was moving slowly along, picking up small branches and debris from trash receptacles that had been blown over in the storm. Shop owners were sweeping the sidewalks and taking down the plywood covers that had been placed over the glass doors and windows to protect them from flying objects. Walking to the corner, Reynolds laughed, turned to Sue, and pointed in the direction of a pushcart offering hot coffee and fresh rolls.

"What's so funny?" Carter asked.

"It's just good to know that some folks won't let a minor inconvenience like a hurricane interrupt their business," he said, shaking his head. Then they turned and walked back to the center.

Though this emergency was over, the cleanup would go on for several days. Reynolds knew they were entering the height of the hurricane season, which meant that it was only a matter of time before he and his staff were thrown into a similar situation.

Chapter 32

Day 5

Piedmont Medical Center

Emergency Waiting Area

The door-to-door canvas by the police and the sheriff's department during the power outage was quite effective. Once the power was restored, the media and the Health Department had wasted no time in responding to Singleton's request for assistance. Television and radio stations had broadcast hourly news flashes with Singleton's message, asking anyone who had attended the county fair or had bought products from the Warren farm to contact the Health Department or come into the medical center for examinations.

By 1:00 p.m. the waiting room outside the ER was filling up. Collins, Frame, Walden, and the ER staff were all busy taking medical histories. Besides hospital staff, Health Department personnel were brought in to help with the screening. The following hours were spent training the patients. Some were admitted and treated, while others who had bought but not eaten the food were checked and released. The process continued nonstop for the rest of the afternoon and into the early evening. Even with extra staff on duty to deal with the large volume of people that had responded to the warning, the waiting room still overflowed with anxious crowds.

It was 8:00 p.m. when the last patients had been taken care of. Collins checked the waiting room and announced, "Okay, Andy, you and Meg get out of here and go to dinner. I'll finish these last two charts and join you in the cafeteria." Then he looked around and said, "It would have been impossible for us to complete this task without your help and I want to thank all of you for your assistance."

When the Health Department personnel left the area, Collins put the final notation on the last chart and rose wearily from the chair. He walked to the sink in the far corner of the room and washed his hands and face. He combed back his hair and left the ER.

Five minutes later, he walked into the cafeteria and was glad to see that Laura Stewart had joined the others already seated at a table in the middle of the room. He took a tray and slid it along the counter selecting a green salad, roast turkey sandwich, coffee, and a brownie for desert. He paid the woman at the cash register, picked up the tray, and walked to the table.

Laura looked up as he approached and, glancing at the other two, she said, "You three have had quite a day, from what I hear. You all look beat."

"We are," he answered, putting his tray on the table and pulling his chair in place. "But it's a nice beat. After Singleton's conference, all the media attention, and the storm thrown in for excitement, I'm surprised we're not still in the ER running cases. Of course we could get more as the news spreads, but I think the worst is over. For now, I just want to sit and enjoy this sandwich, I'm starved."

"We hear you," chorused Walden and Frame, biting into their sandwiches. Looking up, they saw Charlie Bennett walk in grinning from ear to ear. Collins stood and patting Charlie on the back said, "Congratulations, Dad. How are Momma and the baby? You'll have lots of sleepless night for a while," he smiled.

"Everyone is fine, and I was surprised at how well I held up in the delivery room," Charlie said sitting down with a sigh.

It was past midnight when Collins arrived home. A long steamy shower, clean clothes, and a few hours of solid sleep made a world of difference. When the alarm had gone off, he woke refreshed and actually had an hour to talk to Kate and his children. With Katlin on his lap and the boys seated at the table, he asked over her head. "How did all of you do in the storm?"

"I was very brave, Daddy," Katlin piped up. "I didn't cry much, and we played lots of games by candlelight while the power was out."

"That's my brave girl," he said, kissing her on the head. "I knew you would do well. What about you boys?"

"Aw, Dad, it was no big deal," said Danny.

"Yeah," echoed Alexander. "We wanted it to last longer."

"Well, I'm sorry you were disappointed, maybe next time. Now, I want you all to run and play," he laughed, ruffling the boys' heads. "I have to go back to the hospital but I'll see you tonight."

Katlin kissed him on the cheek, and the boys hugged him as he and Kate walked to the door. "So, will you really be home for dinner?" Kate asked.

"Yes, it should be a normal day." Kissing her, he walked out the door to the car.

"I'll fix something special tonight," Kate called after him.

"Thanks," he said. Waving he got into his car and headed back to the hospital.

Chapter 33

Day 6

Offices of Agrotex Research Laboratories

The meeting with Agrotex took Ken Sterling over Afton Mountain. He never tired of the view of the Blue Ridge Mountains rising serenely on all sides. Spread below him were farms and small towns that made up the valley, and as he wove his way through the mountains he caught the reflection of the sun as it glinted off ponds and streams. Around him were the remains of the debris--downed trees and mud covered roads--left by Hurricane Flora. Leaving the highway, he drove a short distance to Agrotex, where he parked in the visitor's lot and got out of the car.

The last time he was here, it had been pouring, but today the sun was shining, and everything seemed peaceful.

Here in the shadow of the Blue Ridge Mountains, away from the city, the air was cool. The trees swayed in the gentle breeze and bees buzzed among the fragrant flowers that lined the walk to the main entrance. He looked again towards the mountains and entered the building.

Though he was early, Sterling was surprised to see that the Virginia Cooperative Extension people were already here. He nodded a greeting and signed in at the desk. Helping himself to a cup of coffee from a carafe set up on a corner table, he walked over to the men and the women who were enjoying the view.

The coffee was hot and strong, and he drank it black. What would we do with out coffee, he thought? As he sipped from the cup, he went over in his mind the brief conversation he'd had last evening with Tyler Wilson. Anxious for this meeting to begin, he finished his coffee and tossed the cup into a nearby waste container. He hoped that, between the Extension people, his office, and those involved here at Agrotex, this matter could at last be resolved.

It was 8:30 a.m. when Wilson's secretary came into the reception area and asked them to accompany her to the small conference room located next to Wilson's office. She followed them in and closed the door behind her.

Two hours later they emerged, amazed and worried about the report that Wilson had given them concerning the incredible and totally unpredictable event that had produced this deadly illness.

Wilson had told them that although every precaution had been taken during the test to ensure the safety and accuracy of the program, no one could have anticipated the bizarre change that occurred to the bacteria culture. He explained that great care was used in selecting the host bacteria to be cultured. This was meant to ensure that its spore- producing capability had been disabled.

What no one had considered possible was the action of the hormones on the bacteria along with the temperature change acting as a catalyst. This combination somehow repaired the defect in the spore-producing gene, enabling it to protect itself again from the effects of cold, heat, and lack of oxygen. Wilson had looked grim in reporting these facts. No doubt, Sterling thought, the man was thinking of the tremendous suffering and alarm this project had caused, and the long-range effect it might have on the company.

Before leaving Sterling stopped briefly to call Laura Stewart and tell her that he was on the way in with a bombshell, and that he would fill her and the others in as soon as he arrived.

Laura had stayed late at the hospital. Before dawn she left and drove home to shower and change clothes. As she came back along US 53, the sun was shining and the air was pine-scented after the storm. Quite a change from the other night, she had thought. Then, it had been so dark and wet every mile had seemed like five. She moved over the winding mountain road quickly. Twenty minutes later she was back at the Medical Center, just in time to catch Ken Sterling's call.

Forty-five minutes later, Sterling pulled into the staff parking lot and went straight to the IDC lab. Laura was waiting for him, having called Collins, Frame, and Singleton to come to the lab.

As Sterling related the information, Laura listened in amazement. When Sterling finished she asked excitedly, "Ken! Have they accounted for all the original culture and grain samples?"

"They believe so, Laura. They're concentrating all their efforts on determining how such a reaction could have occurred in what was supposed to be an irreparable gene condition. Tyler Wilson told us that he's overseeing the project personally."

"Excuse me," interjected Andy. "This is just a little bit over my head. How bad are we talking here?"

"Let me try to explain." said Laura. "As you know, Andy, the most common way to develop a culture is to introduce a common bacterium into an agar or meat-based solution, and let the bacteria produce the hormones or whatever they are grown for. The bacteria used for this purpose cannot produce spores to protect the bacteria from the elements that would normally destroy it, such as heat or cold. This assures that the substance sprayed or treated with culture is not subjected to live bacteria. In this case, it would have been the grain. If I fully understand what Ken has told us, through some improbable circumstance, the introduction of the combination of hormones introduced into the bacteria culture and the temperature deviation repaired the damaged genes, and that's when the trouble started. Ironically, the clue to the answer, and what we overlooked, was that Agrotex's first test was run with sterile, lab birds."

"Why is that important?" asked Frame, unable to contain his curiosity.

Laura continued, "The intestines of the sterile chickens would not have contained the C. jejune bacterium. Therefore no gene transfer occurred. When the folks at Agrotex applied culture to the grain, they were sure that the bacteria it contained were dead. What they apparently did not detect was the presence of live spores that allowed the production of new bacteria after the cells were sterilized."

"I bet that's one lesson the folks at Agrotex won't forget in a hurry." Collins said, standing up and walking to the window. "Sometimes I think we spend so much time looking at what's there, we forget to look at what's missing."

"You're right, Wayne, and we may never know for sure why it happened. I would guess it was some type of gene exchange between the cultured bacteria and the C. jejune strain normally found in chickens that caused the problem. It's something that the CDC and Agrotex will be working on for some time. What makes it so frightening is that this event was brought on by an action thought to be genetically impossible. It's a sobering reminder that nature is capable of reacting in ways that will force us into situations not yet even considered. Hopefully, we'll learn from this experience and move forward. Thank God, we caught this one in time."

"You know, Laura, there's still one thing I don't quite understand," Frame said.

"What's that, Andy?"

"Why were people like the Ryman girl and others who only ate the eggs and not the chicken affected?"

"Well, Andy, from the tests that they ran in Atlanta it would seem that the affected bacteria containing the hormones and other agents used to treat the grain passed from the birds into the embryo of the eggs, and although somewhat less virulent, they were still able to cause serious illness."

"Fortunately, this time the exposure was limited," Collins said as he stared out the window. "The question now is, where will it happen the next time, and how ready will we be?"

Chapter 34

Day 6

Piedmont Medical Center

Going Home

Five days after being brought into the emergency room, Kelly Ryman was packing her few personal belongings into a small overnight bag and preparing for the trip home. She was in the private room to which Doctor Stewart had arranged to have her moved. As she packed, she remembered how frightened she had felt the night she arrived. She could still hear the ambulance siren, and she remembered the bright lights of the examining room, then being surrounded by doctors and nurses all seeming to talk at once. All she had been able to think of was her unborn child.

Sitting on the bed, Kelly looked about the room. This was much nicer, she thought, remembering the long hours in the isolation ward, half delirious, and being fed through IV tubes.

Now it all seemed so unreal. Her illness, the emergency C-section, and the fear that she might never see the baby or Bobby again. It was like waking suddenly from a bad dream.

Tearfully, she recalled the concern on the faces of Doctors Collins and Stewart as they assured her that everything possible would be done for her safety and that of her child. Doctor Stewart, especially, had been so kind to her. She had given daily reports on the baby, and told her how often Bobby had visited during the time that she had been unsure that she would ever completely wake up again. Even arranging for this private room so that she could be alone with the two of them. She looked up as the floor nurse entered the room with the baby, followed by Bobby.

"All set?" the nurse asked Kelly.

"I certainly am," she replied. "But I have a favor to ask before we go."

"What's that, Kelly?" asked the nurse.

"I'd like to stop by the emergency room," Kelly said as a wheelchair was brought into the room. "Doctor Collins has been checking on both of us and I want to thank him and say good-bye."

"I'm sure it would be okay. I'll call down and see if he's available."

"And Doctor Stewart," Kelly said. "Is there any way I could. . ." Her words were interrupted by a knock at the door.

"Did I hear my name?" said Laura, peeking in. "I wanted to see you before you went home, and to say good-bye."

"Thank you, Doctor Stewart, for all you've done for us," said Kelly.

"No, Kelly it's I who should be thanking you and Bobby, too, for what you've done for me."

Looking questionably at Laura, Kelly said, "I don't understand, Doctor Stewart."

"It doesn't matter," Laura said smiling. "The best gratitude you and Bobby could show me is to take care of each other and be happy."

"Thank you, we will," Kelly promised. "We want to stop at the ER to say good-bye to Doctor Collins."

"I'm sure he'd like that Kelly," Laura said squeezing her hand. "Right now, I have a visit of my own to make."

Chapter 35

Day 6

Piedmont Medical Center

Maternity Ward

Amanda Bennett sat up in bed and cuddled her new baby girl close to her chest. Deborah curled her tiny hand around her mother's finger and pulled on her bottle of formula. The downy crown of the baby's head rested snugly in Amanda's arms as she talked to the newest addition to their family. Yesterday Charlie had brought the twins in to see their new sister. After being kings of the hill for ten years, Amanda was afraid that Steve and Tom might resent the baby, but her fears were unwarranted. The boys had come to the hospital with toys and hair ribbons and couldn't wait to see which one of them would be first to hold their new baby sister. Charlie had settled the dispute by putting Deborah on the bed between them so each could hold one of her hands. As the baby finished her formula and Amanda put her over her shoulder to burp, the door of the hospital room opened and a large bouquet of balloons appeared.

"What's this?" asked Amanda, trying to see around the balloons.

"A very proud husband, and dad," answered Charlie, "here to escort two very special ladies home. Are you ready for this, Amanda?"

"Yes, Charlie, we're both ready," she laughed, watching Charlie struggle to set the balloons down.

"While the twins and I load the car, why don't you both get dressed, and we'll be on our way."

"You brought the boys? I thought you left them with Mrs. Johansson," said Amanda, getting up.

"They wanted to come with me," Charlie answered, "and I saw no reason to leave them behind. Right now they're in the gift shop buying one little thing more for Deborah's homecoming. I don't know who's going to spoil our little girl more, Steve or Tom."

Charlie smiled, taking the baby from Amanda and kissing her tiny face.

A nurse entered the room and took the baby while Amanda dressed and gathered her belongings into a small travel case. Charlie picked up the bundle of toys, gifts, and balloons and took them out to the car. With the nurse's help Amanda changed Deborah's diaper and slipped a pink romper over her head. They were both ready and waiting when the twins burst into the room, eager to show their sister the soft purple teddy bear they'd just purchased. Behind them came the floor nurse with instructions for Amanda and a wheelchair.

"I can walk," said Amanda, looking at the chair.

"I'm sure you can, Mrs. Bennett, but it's hospital policy to wheel you out, and I get to carry the baby to the front door," said the nurse, carefully taking the baby into her arms.

Amanda sat in the wheelchair and looked around the room. Charlie was back, and he and the twins gathered around the wheelchair. "I'm afraid the trip home, won't be as exciting as the one in," said Charlie, as they all made their way to the lobby and out to the car waiting at the hospital's main entrance.

"That's fine with me, I've had enough excitement for a while," laughed Amanda.

Chapter 36

Day 6

Piedmont Medical Center

Bill Stewart's Room

When Laura walked into her husband's room, he was reading a travel magazine. The cut over his left eye was beginning to heal. The cast on his left wrist would remain for at least four weeks, and the broken ribs would take time healing. When Bill saw her, he put down the magazine. As she sat down on the side of the bed, he reached out and took her hand. She leaned over and kissed him.

"You're looking better every day," she said.

"So are you," he said, squeezing her hand. "I do feel better. I just have to remember not to move too quickly and jar the ribs. Before you know it, the accident will only be a footnote in my life. The doctor says they're letting me out of here tomorrow."

Then Bill looked more serious. "I just wish somebody could say the same for you."

Laura nuzzled his cheek and said, "I can say it for myself. The epidemic appears to be contained, and things are beginning to get back to normal after the storm. Most of the patients have either left or will in a day or two. Then I'll be all yours."

"And about time, too," Bill answered gruffly as he pulled her closer and kissed her.

"Have you given any more thought to that vacation in Mexico?" Laura asked.

Bill grinned. "I've been lying here thinking about us, and Mexico sounds great. I even saw an article in this magazine that tells all about the rock prospecting possibilities in Mexico."

"I can see this is going to be a very interesting trip," Laura said, smiling back. "While you're recuperating, we can lay out a plan of what else we want to see and do on our trip to Mexico. As soon as you're well enough, we'll buy those tickets. But for now, let's just concentrate on getting you home."

"And you, too."

"Yes," Laura agreed with a laugh, "and me, too."

Chapter 37

Day 6

Piedmont Medical Center

Emergency Room

Andy Frame placed a dressing over the stitches he had just put in Eddie Chafe's leg. The eight-year-old had taken a fall from his bicycle and opened a two-inch gash on his right thigh. The boy's mother stood at the examining table and answered questions while Frame, with the aid of Meg Walden, cleaned the leg and applied a local anesthetic.

Frame then pulled the flesh together with fifteen stitches. Through it all the brown haired boy, his dark eyes solemn, lay quietly. Noting the anxiety on the boy's face Frame said softly, "You know, Eddie, when I was just about your age, I took a pretty good fall too, only mine was off a horse. I had to get a few stitches then and when it was over it wasn't nearly as bad as I expected. I don't know who felt worse, my horse or me," and he watched the smile cross Eddie's face. Finishing up, Frame patted him on the head and said, "Just one more thing, sport, we have to give you a tetanus shot."

Mrs. Chafe put an arm around her son's shoulder while the shot was given, then thanked Frame as Walden gave her an instruction sheet for the care of Eddie's leg.

"You can come back here or go to your family doctor to have the stitches removed," Walden told her as she and Eddie left the ER.

"I wish all our mornings here were so simple," sighed Frame, watching the boy walk away, favoring his injured leg.

Putting away the sterile gauze and dressing, Meg turned to Frame and asked, "Isn't your rotation in the ER up soon, Andy? Have you decided which field you're going into when you finish here?"

"I've pretty much decided on emergency medicine. I've asked Doctor Collins to consider me for a fellowship on his staff, but I haven't gotten a reply yet."

"It's been pretty crazy around here, and he probably hasn't had much time to think about it," Walden said encouragingly.

"Who hasn't had time to think about what?" Collins asked, coming into the ER unnoticed.

"You, and the request I made when this whole thing began."

Collins laughed out loud. "Direct as usual, Andy. I thought maybe after the events of the past week, you might be rethinking your decision concerning emergency medicine."

"Not on your life, if anything I think my outlook on medicine and what it means to be a doctor has become a lot clearer. Those first few days when nothing we did seemed to work made me realize how much we don't know, and just how unpredictable life is. All in all, it was a pretty sobering experience, one I won't forget for a long time."

"Well, I've given your request a lot of thought, and this past week has given me a good opportunity to observe you under pressure. I've also checked your records, and if you think you still want emergency medicine, I would be happy to have you on my team. Will that suit you?" he asked with a broad grin.

"That will suit me fine, and thank you," Frame said, shaking Collins' hand hard.

"Now that that's taken care of, what else is going on here?" Collins asked. "Has it been this quiet all morning?"

"We just finished a minor bicycle accident, which Andy stitched up neatly," said Walden. "Other than that, it's been quiet." She picked up the charts they had started on Eddie Chafe and went to the nurses' station to finish entering the information. She sat for some minutes, and when Collins walked away, she went across the room to Frame. Her green eyes sparkling with curiosity, she said, "Congratulations on getting your fellowship."

"Thanks," he answered, grinning from ear to ear. "Beth will be ecstatic. I promised her that if I got the fellowship, we would set a date for the wedding. In fact, I think I'll call her right now. You'll come, won't you?" he asked.

"I'd love to help you celebrate, She looked at the chart she was holding, but she was thinking about the storm, and Michael, the man she had loved and lost so long ago. With this epidemic under control maybe now was the time to start over. She had been on a date with one of the hospital's pharmacists, and she had enjoyed the evening. He was the complete opposite of Michael, with blond hair and light eyes. And he kept calling her, so why not? Life was unpredictable, that was something an ER nurse should know better than anybody else, Meg thought. Then she turned back to Andy and said, "I'll bring a date, too."

"Great," said Andy.

"Meg, before we get back to business, I know that Wayne thanked everyone for all the extra time they put in here the past few days, but I want to add my thanks too. There were times when I thought I just might lose it. Then I'd look around and see you and the others working so hard to keep things going, it renewed my faith."

"That's sweet of you, Andy, but like you said, everyone worked together. Now, go make that call to Beth while the boss is busy," she said looking toward Collins seated at the desk.

For the next hour Collins caught up on paper work that had piled up over the past week. This was the way an administrators' day should go, he mused. He finished the last of the paper work and piled it neatly in the out bin on his desk. Then he stood and stretched his tired muscles. It had been an intensive few days but the worst was over and the sun was shining. He sat back behind the desk as Meg came over with another chart.

"This one is all complete," she said, smiling. "It only needs your signature." Collins signed the chart and put it with the rest of the paper work, then looked up at Meg and asked "What do you think of Andy as an emergency room doctor?"

"He's young, dedicated, and has a real rapport with patients. I think he has the makings of a fine ER doctor," she answered.

They were still reveling in their accomplishment when they were abruptly interrupted by an announcement over the paging system.

"Doctor Collins, please report to the Medical Command Center, stat."

"I knew it couldn't last," he said, leaving his desk for the center. He walked to the far end of the emergency room, where the Medical Command Center was located. He paused beside the dispatcher and asked, "What do we have?"

"Med-Flight One is approaching the pad with a working code," she answered. Collins moved to the radio and listened to the incoming message.

"Med. Comm. This is Med-Flight One."

"Med-Flight One, this is Doctor Collins. Go ahead, please."

"Yes, sir, we're two minutes out. We have a working code in progress. We have the patient intubated, and we're bagging him. CPR is in progress. Advise transportation this will be a hot unload. Copy."

"That's affirmative, Med-Flight One. We'll be waiting for you."

THE BEGINNING

Author's Comments

Today, most health professionals agree that new microbial threats are appearing in alarming and significant numbers, and well-known illnesses previously controlled are reemerging. Recent facts indicate that there has been a broad resurgence of infectious disease throughout the world. These include major outbreaks of illnesses long thought to be extinct, such as malaria, cholera and diphtheria. Also significant is the alarming emergence of new illness caused by antibiotic-resistant bacteria.

The science of Genetic Engineering is emerging as one of the major weapons in today's medical arsenal. Its effectiveness may, however, be measured by how and where it is applied. Of major concern to the medical community are the new, or reemerging strains of multi-drug-resistant infectious diseases, such as TB and diarrheal diseases caused by parasites and certain strains of E.coli bacteria. It is estimated that of the several billions of dollars lost each year due to illnesses caused by common infectious diseases, intestinal infections and food borne diseases account for more then 23 billion dollars in direct medical costs and lost productivity.

Antibiotic resistance is the price paid for the twentieth century's success against invading microbes. The over use of drugs has reduced their ability to destroy many microbe caused infections, often times resulting in the creation of a new super germ. As these germs multiply they can exchange genetic material with other organisms, transferring to them, the ability to withstand the antibiotic and creating a new resistant strain.

Complicating this has been the frequent use of powerful antibiotic drugs against colds and viral related infections that are not inhibited by such drugs. An example of this was penicillin, the wonder drug of the forties that effectively killed all staph infections. Within the decade many strains had already developed a resistance to it, due in the opinion of many medical researchers, to it's over use. The same pattern developed with methicillin in the sixties.

In the past twenty-five years several new pathogenic microbes as well as infectious diseases have been identified. Meanwhile, the number of new antibiotics introduced into the United States market has declined.

The worldwide medical community has expressed grave concern over the growing number of antibiotic-resistant bacteria appearing almost on a daily basis. Most frightening now is the growing resistance to the drug Vancomycin, which was considered to be the last defense against the growing virulence of staphylococcus and other bacterial infections.

This alone is alarming, as statistics indicate that of the approximately, two-million Staph cases that occur in and out of hospitals each year it is estimated that currently 60,000 to 80,000 people die. It is also feared that other once benign intestinal bacterium such as the now vancomycin-resistant E. faecalis strain, will soon deliver strong Vancomycin resistance to other pathogens making them incurable.

A gastrointestinal bacterium identified as enterococcus was thought to be harmless until it began to mutate out of reach of all drugs including Vancomycin, considered since its introduction in 1958 to be the most powerful antibiotic ever developed. It is hoped that new drugs such as Synercid recently released, and Zyvox currently being tested will prove effective against some of these super microbes but as of now...

In the race between drug-resistant bacteria and new drugs, it appears the bacteria are winning.